CHRISTMAS SURPRISE

Emmy's Story, Part 17

by
Kenneth Lee McGee

For Janae and Andy

Thank you for your faithfulness to the church,
and your support of my stories.
Thank you, Janae, for understanding
my weird sense of humor.

I would like to thank everyone who has taken time to visit
my website or my Amazon author page.
I appreciate the support
and kind words.

I want to thank my wife for coming up the the title.

Chapter One

"Mom, we have to talk right now and this is serious," Heather Rose Colwell said as she and her twin sister, Isabella Marie, trapped their mother in the laundry room by standing in the doorway with their hands on their hips.

Emmy Colasanti-Colwell tossed the last of the dirty towels into the washer, added a packet of detergent, closed the lid, punched the button to start the machine and turned around. "What did your brother do now?"

Heather shook her head. "Kevin Michael didn't do anything, but this concerns him, too. We talked about this, and we're all in agreement."

Emmy leaned against the washer and took a deep breath. "Okay, tell me what's on your mind."

"We want separate rooms!" Heather and Isabella shouted simultaneously.

Kevin Michael Colwell pushed between his sisters and entered the room. "Yeah! I want to switch rooms. I want the nanny suite since it's always empty. That way I will have a separate entrance from the garage and can have all my friends over without anyone knowing."

Emmy shook her head. "No way! You're only ten. The nanny suite is reserved for guests and Father James if he is ever allowed to retire."

"I talked to Uncle James, and he said he wasn't going to use it for several years if ever," Kevin said. "He said he might have to stay a priest until he's like ninety or older."

Emmy tried to scoot past the kids, but Heather and Isabella stood beside their younger brother like a football line guarding the quarterback and didn't allow her to get past.

"Mom! We are totally serious about this," Isabella said. "We have a plan that will work."

Emmy stared at the quietest and most serious of her children and leaned against the counter where a pile of clean clothes waited to be folded. "Okay, let me hear your plan."

Isabella continued, "We've outgrown the playroom, so

1

Kevin could move in there. Then Heather and I could have the bedrooms on the same side of the hall."

"You would still have the guest bedroom like it is now, and keep the nanny suite totally empty and wasted space like you insist," Heather said sarcastically.

"Go on," Emmy said folding her arms over her chest. "I assume there is more."

The twins nodded and Kevin grinned mischievously.

"Spill it," Emmy said and then sighed. "I have a feeling this is going to cost me some money."

"Not too much, but we want to paint the bedrooms a more grownup color and get rid of all the kid stuff like the stars on the ceiling," Heather explained.

"I want to paint my new bedroom black," Kevin said.

"Not a chance," Emmy quashed that plan immediately.

"Well, something other than what it is now, and we have to get rid of that mural. It's for babies."

"It's not for babies," Emmy insisted. "It's based on a Bible story for children."

"Exactly," Kevin said.

"I suppose you can paint the rooms, but I have final approval of all color choices."

The kids huddled together to discuss their mother's offer.

Heather said, "Deal, but we have one more request that is not up for debate whatsoever."

"I'm listening," Emmy said. *This is what's going to cost an arm and a leg.*

"We need new bedroom sets," Heather said. "Isa and I are using the same beds we've had since we got out of baby cribs. We need new queen-sized beds, and new dressers like you and Daddy have."

"Nightstands, too," Isabella added.

"You aren't using the same beds you had when you were little," Emmy said without much confidence. "Are you?"

The twins nodded.

"We barely fit on them anymore," Isabella said. "If we get new beds now, they should last until we go to college."

"You aren't going to college for a long time."

"Mom, we will be in eighth grade in the fall. Five years after that is college," Heather said.

"That can't be possible," Emmy said.

"It's okay, Mom, you're not getting older. We are," Kevin said putting an arm around her shoulders.

"Nice try, buddy, and when did you grow as tall as me?"

"I'm probably taller, Mom. I'm still growing, and you stopped a long, long time ago."

"How do you know?" Emmy asked poking him in the side playfully.

"Dad said so. He said you were this tall when you got to junior high and never grew another inch."

"Mom, it's okay that you're height challenged. We love you anyway," Heather said. "Can we go ahead with our plans? It's not like it should matter to you or Daddy since you have the whole end of the upstairs to yourselves."

Emmy bit her lip for a moment, then nodded. "I will talk to your father tonight."

The girls giggled and Heather said, "That's okay. We already asked him, and he said he would go along with whatever you decided."

"You're getting too sneaky," Emmy said. *You remind me of myself in that way.*

The kids raced out of the room, sprinted through the kitchen, down the wide hallway, past the stairs going to the second floor and turned into the family room where their father, Kenny Colwell, was sitting in his new, black leather recliner talking to Andy Walker, who managed Kenny's band, Fridays At Five.

"Daddy! Mom said we could do it!" Heather shouted as she plopped onto his lap nearly knocking the recliner over.

"Do what?" he asked.

"Switch rooms, paint them and get new bedroom sets," Isabella explained while sitting next to Andy on the couch.

Andy put his arm around Isabella's shoulders, gave her a gentle squeeze and said, "You are getting prettier everyday."

Kevin sprawled out in one of the other recliners and stared

at the giant TV on the wall.

"Oh, you were serious about that, huh?" Dad asked.

"Yes, and you know we were serious. When can we pick out the paint and the new furniture? We want to make the change before we go back to school."

Emmy walked into the room carrying a basket of folded laundry. "Someone has to take this upstairs. I'm getting too old to carry it. I'm thirty-eight and that's close to forty. You might have to put me in a nursing home before the end of the year."

"Mom, you do know there is a laundry room upstairs, right?" Kevin asked. "It's at the end of the hall right before the nanny suite."

"I know, but that washer needs to be replaced. It doesn't work right, and I have to bring everything down here anyway." Emmy set the basket on the coffee table and sat on the couch next to Andy. "Did you know about this?"

"About what, cuz? I'm totally innocent in the matter," Andy claimed a bit too loudly.

"Yeah, right," Emmy said rolling her eyes. "You probably let them see the new furniture you bought for Christmas and gave them the idea. I should make you pay for everything."

"They could really use bigger beds," Kenny said.

"Yes!" Kevin jumped up and hollered. "I want one of those beds that hang from the ceiling, so I have extra room underneath for a desk and all my gear."

"Can we pick out the paint and furniture today?" Heather asked jumping up and pulling on her father's hands. "I'm sure the stores are open and probably have great sales since it's after the holidays."

Kenny looked at Emmy and tilted his head.

She rolled her eyes. "Fine! I know when to surrender. Can you take them?"

Kenny shrugged and said, "I could, but I'm a poor judge of paint color and wouldn't have a clue about furniture."

Emmy stood up and kicked Andy's foot. "I should make you go with us since this is all your fault."

"I would go, but Kenny and I have to discuss important

4

band business. Then we need to visit Jeff and see how he's doing. Heart attacks are serious business. Remember? I had one fifteen years ago."

"I remember and you survived," Emmy smiled at Kenny using her best I-will-make-it-worth-your-while-later expression, but it didn't matter. Kenny didn't cave. "Fine! I will take the kids after I shower and get dressed, but I better not hear any complaints when you get the Visa bill."

"You can't wear that if you're going to help paint," Emmy ordered pointing to the new top Heather was wearing. "Find some old sweatshirt or something that won't matter if you get paint all over it."

Tony Bertucci walked into the room, put his hands on Emmy's shoulders and teased, "Am I supposed to carry you out of the room, too?"

"Don't you dare!" Emmy turned to face one of her best friends, who lived across the road with his family of six kids, a wife, his mother and a dog named Scout. "Did everything fit into the nanny suite?"

"The only thing left to move is that bookcase, and I will move it as soon as someone empties all those books."

"Uncle Tony, can't you carry it with the books still there?" Isabella asked sweetly. "You're big and strong because you used to play football for the Bears."

"He might have been in shape then," Emmy poked him in the stomach and laughed. "But look at him now. He's all flabby and soft. I doubt he could lift me."

Tony shook his head. "I'm in good enough shape to play right now if I wanted. I'll carry it with the books if you want, Isa."

Tony carried the bookcase to the nanny suite and only dropped a few books along the way.

"What are you looking at, Em?" Kenny asked walking into the room.

"Should we replace the carpeting since the room is empty?"

"It still looks good," Kenny said. He squatted and rubbed the carpeting. "If we had the time, I'd like to put in hardwood like the hallway and our room. These bedrooms are the only rooms in the house that still have carpeting."

"Other than the basement, you mean, right?" Emmy added.

"I like the carpeting, Daddy," Isabella said. "It's warmer than the hardwood."

"What time are the painters coming?" Tony asked returning to the room.

Kenny checked his phone. "They should be here soon."

"Should we let them do it all?" Emmy asked. "They can probably get everything done by the time the kids and I finish one wall."

"I want to help a little," Heather said. She walked into the room wearing an old Notre Dame sweatshirt.

Emmy saw her and shook her head. "No way you are wearing that. Put it back." Emmy pointed toward the master bedroom suite.

"You said to find something old, and this is like thirty years old," Heather said with a grin.

"It might be old, but I still like to wear it and you know it," Emmy said about the sweatshirt Tony had given her many years ago.

The painters arrived ten minutes later and within two hours all three bedrooms had new coats of paint.

"Well, how do you like the color, Em?" Kenny asked.

"I should have known Isa would pick a shade of purple. I wish I could have had a room like this when I was young."

After letting the paint dry, Tony, Kenny and Emmy's nearly seventeen-year-old nephew, Carson Garrett, moved the furniture that would be staying in the bedrooms back into place.

"Where are the kids going to sleep tonight?" Tony asked.

"I'm sleeping at your house," Kevin Michael answered. "Ben and I are going to camp in the backyard. We might let Taylor camp, too, but he said it might be too cold."

"At last Taylor has some sense," Emmy said. "It's too cold to camp outside."

"Can we make a fort in the basement?" Kevin asked.

"You have to ask Sloane. Don't ask this guy because he

6

might want to join you." Emmy bumped hips with Tony.

"Where are the girls sleeping? I suppose they can sleep in the nanny suite," Kenny said. "We didn't put anything in the bedroom. It all fit in the sitting room."

Isabella put her arms around her father's waist and hugged him. "We're having a slumber party at Uncle Tony's house. Noemi and Grace said we could do that."

"Are you inviting Dotty?" Tony asked.

"Noemi asked if she wanted to join us, but Dotty said no. She didn't want to go to a slumber party with junior high girls." Heather put a hand on her hip and rocked it back and forth. "Just because she goes to high school at that snooty old Barclay Academy, she thinks she's so cool."

"You and Isa might be joining Dotty at that snooty old school," Emmy said.

"I'd rather go to Reagan or St. Raymond's than go there," Heather said.

"We will cross that bridge when we get there," Kenny replied ending the discussion.

"I think I heard the truck," Kevin shouted the next morning as he dashed through the kitchen. He opened the door to the mudroom, slid across the floor, entered the garage, flew down the steps, raced to the service door and stepped outside just as the delivery truck from Turk Brothers Furniture braked to a squeaky stop. He waited until the men exited the truck.

"Is this where all this stuff gets delivered?" the driver, Frank Turk, asked.

"Yeah! I'll open one of the garage doors, and you can use the back staircase. That will be easier than going through the house."

The driver's helper stared at the three double-wide garage doors and asked, "You ever been here before?"

"Several times," Frank answered. "Big place, huh?"

"He's a famous rock star, right?"

"Yeah, but you'd never know it if you met him on the street. He's just a local SoHam guy who did all right for himself."

7

Emmy walked through the garage and opened one of the overhead doors. "Hello, Frank. Kenny moved the cars, so you could have a straight shot up the stairs. Did Kevin explain that already?"

"He did, Emmy, and Uncle Franklin wanted me to make sure you know how much he appreciates the business."

"I understand times can be tough for local businesses with all the chain stores and online shopping available now. We've always been more than satisfied with the stuff we buy from you guys. Grandma Isabel bought her furniture from you for over fifty years."

Kenny joined them outside. "Do you need any help, Frank? I can carry stuff, and Tony said he would help if we need him."

"Thanks, but we're good, Mr. Colwell," Frank said.

Kenny showed them the back stairs leading to the nanny suite. "There's a clear path through the sitting room to the hallway."

Frank and his helper took a look.

"Those are some wide stairs," the helper whispered to Frank.

"I think they planned ahead."

"Emmy will be upstairs to show you where everything goes," Kenny said.

In under ninety minutes, all the new furniture had been assembled and moved into place in all three bedrooms.

"Uncle Franklin said you had some furniture going back to the store," Frank said as he and Emmy walked into the nanny suite. "Is this it, Emmy?"

"We don't have any use for this anymore. I told your uncle he could either sell it or donate it to a good cause."

Soon the nanny suite was emptied of the kids' old furniture.

As Frank closed the back door of the truck and then jumped down, Emmy shoved some money into his pocket. "I know your uncle has rules against tipping the deliverymen, but you know I never listen to him. You can share this with your helper."

Frank shook is head. "I know better than to argue with you, Emmy. You're more stubborn than me or Uncle Franklin. Thanks

8

for this and thank you for the used furniture. It still looks in good shape."

"It should be. We bought it from your store," Emmy said with a grin as she headed inside.

She walked upstairs, through the nanny suite, into the hallway and saw the girls dashing in and out of their bedrooms.

"Oh, Mommy! We love our new rooms and our new beds and all the other furniture," Isabella exclaimed as she hugged her mother tightly. "Thank you so much. Even Kevin Michael loves his new room even though he has to share the bathroom with the guest bedroom."

"I'm glad you like it. You have to take care of it so it lasts a long time. Maybe when you grow up and have your own place, you can take it with you," Emmy said kissing the top of Isabella's head.

"That's a long way off," Isabella said and then dashed into her new room.

Emmy bit her lip. *I hope it's a long time off, but you are growing up way too fast as far as I'm concerned. You were just babies a little while ago.*

Heather and Isabella hurried to their Sunday School classroom at church the next morning. They spotted Noemi Bertucci talking to her cousin Grace Randolph and Natalie Hammond, the older daughter of Pastor Tyler and Liz, and rushed to talk to them.

"We slept in our new rooms last night," Heather interrupted. "We finally have separate bedrooms. Isn't that just the edge of danger?"

"I've always had my own room," Grace said.

Natalie and Noemi nodded.

"We've always shared a room," Isabella said.

"Aren't there lots of bedrooms in your house?" Natalie asked.

"Yeah, but we've always shared a room. It was all right when we were younger, but we need our privacy now," Heather explained. "We will be teenagers next Sunday."

9

"Mr. Kesson! You're back!" Emmy exclaimed as she and Kenny entered the spacious office on the second floor of the Steward Music Group headquarters Monday morning. She immediately noticed the platinum records had been placed back on the walls. She turned and saw a pile of books stacked haphazardly on the old, scarred wooden desk. Several LPs were stacked against a stand with a turntable and stereo system on top. "It's good to see you again. How have you been?"

Max Kesson, dressed in his customary faded jeans and plaid flannel shirt, set a folder down, stood up and walked out from behind his desk. He scratched his beard and then smiled. "It's good to be back to work. I was getting bored sailing around the Caribbean without a goal other than working on my tan." He shook hands with Kenny and hugged Emmy. "I'd much rather be trying to discover new bands to record."

"It's good to have you back," Kenny said.

Andy Walker entered the room, walked over to the worn couch and sat down. "My back has been killing me. I never should have tried to drag the Christmas tree out to the street."

Emmy shook her head. "You could have asked one of the kids to do it for you."

Mr. Kesson sat in his worn, comfortable recliner and Kenny and Emmy joined Andy on the couch.

"How are Sheila and the kids?" Emmy asked.

"She is still in Florida with the grandkids. My daughters are in Colorado skiing. Norah and her husband split up last year. Can't say I blame her. He was about as useful as salt in the desert."

Kenny and Andy looked at each other and then at Mr. Kesson.

Mr. Kesson waved. "You want to know about Klaus, huh?"

Andy nodded.

"I made a mistake," Mr. Kesson said. "Two of them actually. First, I thought he was ready to take over the business. He wasn't. He didn't share my love for music, and he was too interested in expanding into movies and becoming some kind of mogul. Second, he didn't understand the most valuable assets of this company are the artists."

10

"He did have some strange ideas," Kenny said.

"Just so you know, I've closed the entire Los Angeles office, and Klaus is no longer making any decisions involving Steward Music Group. He decided he would rather try his hand at selling real estate in San Francisco."

"Did the company lose money because of Klaus?" Andy asked.

"Doesn't matter. We can now get back to taking care of the artists and creating a better workplace."

"I like that idea," Emmy said.

"So, I read your proposal about a vanity label," Mr. Kesson said looking at Kenny. "I think it's time you start producing some projects that interest you."

Kenny smiled at Emmy and patted her thigh. "Now that Fridays At Five doesn't take up all my time, I need something to inspire my creative process."

Emmy rolled her eyes. "Thought processes my butt! You're just a singer in a rock band who knows how to play a few chords on your guitar."

"He's done all right producing your CDs," Andy said.

"Emmy, I know you aren't obligated to Steward Music for another project, and I know you've shifted your focus to your writing, but would you consider recording one final CD for me?" Mr. Kesson asked.

"I think I might have enough songs for one final project, but could I have a professional producer this time? I've been sleeping with my old producer, and he's gotten lazy over the years." She elbowed Kenny's side.

"I put in a lot of time on your projects, Em." He rubbed his side.

"I'll ask Stuart Lederer if he's got time to work with you," Mr. Kesson grinned.

Chapter Two

"Mom!" Kevin Michael hollered walking into his parents bedroom suite. "Do I have to hang around for the party? I want to do something with Ben."

Emmy finished brushing her hair and looked at him. "You don't have to be here tonight for their party, but I'd like you to be here for lunch and when we sing 'Happy Birthday.' You can leave early, but I won't guarantee there'll be any cake left."

"I don't care about birthday cake. I don't want to listen to them yapping about how they're teenagers now." He shrugged and said, "I don't see what the big deal is."

"You'll understand in a couple of years."

"Do I have to watch them open presents?" he asked while making a face.

"It would be nice. They are your sisters, and you do love them."

Kevin rolled his eyes, turned around and hollered over his shoulder while walking out of the room, "I'll do it this year, but forget about next year and in the future."

"Mom! Make Kevin behave! He's trying to embarrass us," Heather hollered as everyone gathered in the family room after lunch to watch the girls open presents. "He's making faces and fart noises. He's such a child."

"Kevin Michael, stop whatever you're doing and behave for a few minutes. This will be over soon enough and then you can play with Ben," Kenny whispered while squeezing Kevin's shoulder.

"I hope someone bought them underwear so I can make fun of them."

"Hush," Kenny insisted.

"Andy, will you please light the candles?" Emmy asked after all the gifts had been opened and everyone squeezed around the kitchen island.

He did and Emmy helped the group start singing. The girls blew out all the candles in one try.

12

"Did you make a wish?" Elly Colwell asked while leaning close to Isabella.

"Yes, but you know I can't tell you, Grandma."

Emmy cut the cake into slices, placed them onto paper plates and handed them to Kenny who scooped out ice cream.

"This is actually pretty good cake. Where did you get it?" Carter Colwell asked while getting a second slice.

"I ordered it from Tobin's Catering. Gina goes to our church, and she makes the best cakes in SoHam," Emmy answered. "Would you like more ice cream, Dad? It appears Kenny has abandoned his post."

"I can get it myself, Emmy. Thank you."

Emmy felt a hand on her shoulder and looked at her half-brother. "Do you want another slice? There's only three left. I should have ordered a larger cake."

Father James shook his head. "I'm good, but I want to show you something." He held her arm and guided her out of the kitchen, across the hall and into the seldom used formal living room. "Have a seat."

She sat and noticed a box of photos scattered on the couch. "Where did you find these?"

"Kenny brought them out of the library. He was looking for a certain photo."

"Which one?"

Father James picked one up and handed it to Emmy. "Do you recognize this person?"

Emmy glanced at the photo. "Of course. It's me. Why?"

Father James grinned and asked, "Does it remind you of anyone?"

Emmy turned the photo over and read the date. "This was taken at Kenny's house the summer I turned thirteen. So what?"

"This is a photo Kenny took of the twins yesterday." He handed it to Emmy.

She compared the photos and sighed.

"You could be triplets," Father James said. "The girls look so much like you at that age. Your hair is longer and maybe more frizzy..."

"Shush!" She poked his arm.

"But they look just like you. Check out their eyes and cheekbones and the nose."

"I am their mother," Emmy said.

"I haven't seen many photographs of you growing up, and of course I wasn't around," he whispered.

"It's no one's fault we didn't know each other," Emmy said. "I can understand why your birth mother didn't let Daddy know he had a son."

"I do believe we met at the time God ordained," Father James said with his fingers intertwined.

Emmy poked his arm. "You can be such a dork at times."

"I am a man of the cloth..."

"Yeah, did I tell you what I heard the girls talking about the other day?"

"Possibly, but remind me."

"I was changing the sheets in Kevin's room and I heard them talking about boys."

"They are teens. It's normal."

"Maybe, but... Oh, never mind."

"No! Tell me."

"It's embarrassing," she whispered.

"Then I must know," he teased.

"Fine! But it might embarrass you."

"I've heard a lot of things during confession. It takes an awful lot to embarrass me now."

"The girls know a lot more about sex than me."

Father James laughed. "I seriously doubt that."

She smacked his arm. "I don't mean now! I meant they know more about sex than I did when I was their age. You knew what I meant."

"You grew up without the Internet and cell phones and social media platforms..."

"Yeah, I get it. I'm ancient."

"They are exposed to a lot more than you were."

"Yeah, I learned everything from Diane and Rory."

Father James stared at her.

She saw his expression and said, "I didn't mean it like that."

"Good to know." Father James turned as someone entered.

"What's going on in here?" Andy Walker asked. "Is this a private conversation? You never use this room. It might as well be closed off and used for storage."

Emmy handed him the photo. "Which one of the twins is that? And don't turn it over to check."

Andy took the photo and examined it quickly. "It has to be Isabella because I can't see the birthmark on Heather's elbow." He handed it back and said smugly, "You can't fool me. I know it all."

Father James chuckled and Emmy grinned. She handed it back.

"What?" Andy asked.

"Look on the back."

He turned it over. "Wait! Is that date correct?"

"Yep," Emmy said.

Andy examined the photo closer. "Okay, now I can see this was taken many years ago. Look at the old-fashioned grill in the corner."

"It wasn't taken that long ago," Emmy said making a face.

"I knew it was you. I was just teasing," Andy said.

"It's a sin to lie," Father James said using his serious priest voice.

"Fine. I was misled by her leading question. She was the one who lied first."

Emmy handed Andy the real photo of the twins. "Can you see a resemblance?"

"Yeah, they look like twins."

"You can be so dense at times," Emmy said with a sigh. "Can you see the resemblance between the girls and me?"

Andy looked at both photos. "Wow! I'm used to you looking the way you do now, but it is difficult to tell you apart from the twins."

Emmy frowned at Andy. "What do you mean by the way I look now? Do I look like an old woman?"

"I'm afraid she's got you there, Andy." Father James stood up. "Excuse me, but I don't want to get in the middle of this fight."

15

"I just meant you don't look thirteen anymore, cuz. You look more like a lady in her mid-twenties."

Emmy stood up and took the photos from Andy. "I'll let you slide for now." She headed back to the kitchen and passed the photos around.

"It's amazing how much they look like you," Kristen Randolph said handing the photos to Sloane Bertucci.

"Let me see those," Tony insisted. He stared at the photos for several seconds before asking, "How old were you when I met you?"

Emmy thought for a second and then faced Tony. "If you mean when you so eloquently introduced yourself in the hallway at Roosevelt High, I was seventeen and a senior. But if you mean when we actually first met, I was four, and we played football in the backyard."

"I meant in high school," Tony said. He touched the tip of her nose and smiled. "You weren't as much of a brat then."

"How many kids are there downstairs?" Kenny asked when Emmy sat next to him in the family room.

"I think there are twenty-five to thirty. Ian Plant is here with his sister, Brienna," Emmy said making Ian's name sound vulgar." Emmy poked Kenny's side and added, "Oh, and I was informed we are not to come downstairs even if the house is on fire."

"Isn't that the boy Heather kissed when she was ten?" Kenny asked setting down his book.

"Yes, and he's fifteen now. You know how fifteen-year-old boys can be, right?"

"I vaguely remember being that age, and I remember this young girl always trying to kiss me." He pulled Emmy onto his lap, held her close and tried to kiss her.

She squirmed away and said, "That wasn't me. You didn't kiss me until I was sixteen at least. Maybe older. You were so shy."

He rubbed his jaw. "Then who was that girl. I remember she was pretty cute and a great kisser."

16

"Hush. Did you lock the studio?"

"No, but I told Isa to keep everyone out of there."

A few minutes later they heard the thump of a heavy bass that vibrated the floor.

"They must have the music pretty loud," Emmy said. "The studio is soundproof. I better go check." She tried to stand up, but Kenny grabbed her hand. "They might blow up some expensive speakers."

He pulled her back onto the couch. "You promised to stay up here. The studio is soundproof, but the rest of the basement isn't. Speakers can be replaced. Let them have some fun."

"They better not be having too much fun," Emmy said. She pulled her knees to her chest and wrapped her arms around them.

"Are you thinking about some of the wild parties you used to sneak out to with Rory Porter?" Kenny asked knowing it would get a response.

"I never did anything at those parties with Rory that I need to feel guilty about."

"Are you sure? I've heard some rumors."

"What rumors?" she asked sitting up straight.

"Certain rumors about what might have happened..."

"You're just fishing for details that don't exist. Rory always treated me like a kid sister."

"His real sister was pretty wild," Kenny mentioned.

Emmy pictured Rory's late sister Amy, who had been murdered in her apartment in 2010.

"She had a rough childhood."

"Are you using that as an excuse for her? Your childhood wasn't exactly without its peaks and valleys."

"Mine was like ice cream and blueberry pie compared to hers. Rory told me their father would do things that Daddy never did."

"Do I want to know?"

"He drank more than Daddy, and he would hit their mother. Rory told me once he threatened to use a baseball bat on his father."

"Did he?"

17

"No, his father left and didn't come back."

"Ever?"

"I guess he would show up at times, but he never lived in the house after that."

"So, Rory has always been a protector, huh?"

She cuddled closer to Kenny and put her head where she could feel his heart beating. "He hid that side of himself from most people, but I knew about his softer side."

"What was that?" Kenny asked after hearing a loud crash.

Emmy jumped up. "I better check. They might have broken a window or one of the light fixtures." She ran out of the family, across the hall to the basement door and stopped. She returned to the couch. "I need to learn to trust the girls. I don't want to be like my mother."

"Your mother had good reason to be a smidge mistrustful," he said.

She smacked his arm.

"Hey! I meant because of Diane. You were a perfect angel at all times."

"Maybe not all the time," she admitted with a gleam in her eyes.

"What time is your parents' flight?" Emmy asked the next morning.

"They need to be at the airport by nine," Kenny answered.

Emmy walked into their bathroom and watched Kenny trying to trim his five-day-old beard. "Are you really going to keep that scrawny thing?"

"Don't you like it?"

"Can I be honest?"

He paused and stared at her.

"I used to think it was sexy when you wouldn't shave for a few days, but with all that gray in your beard it makes you look older than you are."

He leaned closer to the mirror. "There's not that much gray, is there?"

"There's enough to be noticeable."

He turned his head back and forth to check each side. "Fine! I'm shaving it."

"Should I buy you some of that hair stuff that gets rid of gray?" she asked with a grin.

"Someday you'll get old, Em, and your hair won't always look like it does now."

"Maybe but I can always color it and you'll never know," she teased. "How long are your parents going to stay in Florida?"

He shrugged and said, "April for sure but they might stay until May if the weather in SoHam sucks."

"Mom! Mom! Help!" Heather screamed in the middle of the night the next Saturday. "Mommy! I need you," Heather yelled again.

"What's going on?" Kenny asked. He threw back the covers and rolled out of bed.

Emmy jumped up. "I think I know. Stay here. Let me see what's going on. It might be... uh... you know."

"What?" he asked running a hand threw his hair.

"Female stuff," Emmy said while racing out of the room.

"Female stuff," Kenny said while reaching back for the edge of the bed. He missed it and fell to the floor with a thud. He rubbed the back of his head while muttering, "What female stuff?"

Emmy raced past the top of the stairs, grabbed hold of the newel post to help turn the corner and raced down the hallway. She saw Kevin stick his head out of his room, pointed at him and hollered, "Stay in your room."

"What's going on?" he asked.

"Nothing. Stay in your room," Emmy ordered as she entered Heather's room.

Kenny stood up and stubbed his toe trying to get back in bed. He hopped around for a time and bumped into the nightstand before tripping and landing in bed. "It can't be female stuff already. They're babies."

"Mom! I'm bleeding to death," Heather sobbed.

Isabella stepped into the hall and saw her brother's head peeking out.

"Something's wrong," Kevin said as his voice cracked.

Isabella took his arm and led him back into his room. "I'm pretty sure Heather will be all right," she whispered. "If it will help you calm down, we can pray for her."

"Okay," he whispered and sat on the edge of his bed.

Isabella sat beside him.

"Mom!" Heather sobbed holding up a wet, dark red hand.

"Heather, you're going to be okay," Emmy whispered. "We did talk about this. You were having cramps earlier this week, remember?"

Heather wiped her nose with her other hand and nodded.

"I talked to you and Isa about what would happen."

Heather sobbed again.

"I'm not surprised this has happened, You do know what it is, right?"

Heather nodded again.

"We talked about what you need to do."

"I didn't know there would be some much... yuck. I feel sick thinking about it."

"Let's clean you up in the bathroom, and I'll help you with... the thing I told you about."

Ten minutes later Heather climbed back into bed. "Will you stay with me until I fall asleep?"

"Yes, sweetie," Emmy whispered. She slid into bed and put an arm around her daughter's shoulders.

"It's been quiet for several minutes," Kevin whispered to Isabella. "Do you think Heather's okay, or is she dead?"

"She's not dead, you dorkbrain," Isabella said getting off the bed. "Go back to sleep before I clobber you."

Emmy returned to her bed thirty minutes later.

Kenny put an arm around her and asked, "Is Heather all right?"

Emmy cuddled close and whispered, "Her period started and it scared her. She's sleeping now."

"Geez! How can it start so fast? She's just a kid."

"Isabella won't be far behind," Emmy replied.

"Heather, I need to use the bathroom and you have to come with me," Isabella whispered as someone dropped a lunch tray on the other side of the cafeteria.

"Why? I'm not finished with my lunch," Heather answered. "You can go by yourself."

Noemi Bertucci and Natalie Hammond sat across the table finishing their burgers and chips.

Isabella stood up and tugged on Heather's arm. "You need to come with."

"I'm finished," Natalie said. "I can go with you."

"Thanks, Natty, but I really need Heather right now."

Heather took a sip of chocolate milk and looked up at her sister. "Oh, is it your tummy?"

Isabella nodded.

"Noemi, would you take my tray back, please. I need to run."

"I'll take care of it. Go ahead," Noemi answered.

Heather and Isabella rushed away.

"I have to stop at my locker to get my backpack," Isabella said.

"Do you have the... you know... in it?" Heather asked.

"Yes, Mommy told me to be prepared."

"Is Isa sick?" Natalie, in fifth grade, asked as she picked up the trash other students left behind.

"You could say that," Noemi answered.

They walked together to return the trays.

"I hope she feels better. Maybe it was the baked beans. Mine tasted a bit weird."

Heather threw open the bathroom door, checked to see if they were alone and faced Isabella. "Did it start?"

Isabella nodded and opened her backpack. "Did you tell Noemi what happened?" Isabella asked while pulling out the small bag containing everything she needed.

"I mentioned it in English because she was having cramps. She might be getting her period, too." Heather stood guard as Isabella closed the stall door. "Did you bring clean underwear?"

"Yes, should I throw these away?"

21

"Yeah! You can't wear them again. That would be so gross."

By the time Isabella finished, the second bell had rung.

"We are going to be late to math," Isabella said.

"Good thing Aunt Sloane is our teacher. Maybe she won't notice."

Heather and Isabella rushed to their next class, which was on the second floor at the opposite end of the building. They cautiously entered the room and tiptoed toward their desks.

Sloane Bertucci, who had known the twins since birth, looked up from her desk and motioned to the girls.

"Busted!" one of the boys shouted.

Heather and Isabella slowly approached their teacher.

"We're sorry we're late," Isabella said. "It was my fault."

"We were in the bathroom," Heather admitted.

"Are you not feeling well, Isa? Do you need to see the nurse?"

"It's not that," Isabella whispered while listening to some of the kids making fun of her.

"What is the matter?" Sloane asked the class sternly. "Be quiet and open your books. I hope you finished the problems I assigned Friday." She turned back to Isabella. "Do you need to see the nurse?"

Isabella shook her head.

"Can you tell me what's wrong, sweetie?"

Isabella looked at Heather and shook her head.

Heather moved next to Sloane, leaned close and whispered what really caused them to be late.

"I see," Sloane whispered. "Isa, you may go to the nurse if you need, or I could call your mother."

"I'd rather stay if that's okay, Mrs. Bertucci."

"Of course you may stay. Are you feeling better?"

"Yes," Isabella whispered.

She and Heather sat down and Mrs. Bertucci stood and walked to the front of her desk to begin the class.

"Who's picking us up today?" Heather asked after the day's last class. They stopped at their lockers, put their books away and headed outside to wait for their ride.

"Daddy is supposed to pick us up, and Zachary and Grace need a ride, too. Please don't say anything."

"I'm not gonna tell Daddy. Mom told him about me and he freaked. He's such a dork like Mommy calls him."

"I meant don't tell Grace or Zach."

"Like I would tell Zach anything. He's worse than Kevin."

Later, after finishing her homework, Isabella headed to the kitchen where Emmy was trying to decide what to make for dinner.

"Mommy, can I talk to you?" Isabella asked.

Emmy grabbed a bag of frozen ravioli and kicked the freezer door closed. "Sure, Isa. What is it?"

"It's... you know." Isabella backed up to make sure no one was in the hallway listening and pointed to her stomach.

"Oh," Emmy said. "At school?"

Isabella nodded. "At the end of lunch. I made Heather come to the bathroom with me..." Isabella explained what happened.

"Why didn't you tell Sloane? She would have understood."

"I was too embarrassed, but Heather told her."

"Are you all right now? Any cramping or anything?"

"Mom! I don't want to talk about it."

"You don't have to, but I'm always here if you need to talk about something. Anything. Doesn't matter what."

"Thanks, Mom." Isabella started to walk away but stopped. "What should I do with the underwear? Heather told me to throw them away, but I didn't."

Emmy chuckled and put an arm around Isabella. "When it happened to me, I felt like Heather. I threw so much underwear away. After a few times it didn't bother me so much."

"Are you going to tell Daddy?"

"I'll tell him when we go to bed. Hopefully, he won't freak out like he did the other night. Did I tell you he fell and bumped his head and then stubbed his toe. He told me he was hopping around trying to grab the back of his head and his foot at the same time." Emmy laughed and said, "He can be a real dork at times."

"Tell me," Isabella said and then hugged her mother.

Emmy's cell phone chirped just as she sat down at her computer to work on her latest book. Emmy saw who was calling and answered.

"Lynette, how are you. I was thinking about you earlier. I needed some advice and thought about you."

Lynette Jefferson, the wife of the pastor of the small Nazarene church on the east side of South Hampshire, and who had known Emmy for over twenty years, laughed and replied, "It's nice to know you still value my advice. Are you having boyfriend trouble again?" Lynette teased.

"No such luck," Emmy joked. "It's the twins."

"I sent them a birthday card. Did you see it?"

"Yes, it was cute."

"I can't believe they are teenagers already. I still think of them as little girls. What are they up to? Besides school."

"They started their periods. Isabella today and Heather in the middle of Saturday night. Heather freaked out, but Isa handled it like a pro."

"Sounds about right. Isabella has always been down to earth and Heather is the drama queen. My girls are the same way. Ruth is steady as a rock, and Esther can be as flighty as a sparrow caught in a hurricane."

"I haven't seen them in ages. How are they doing?"

"I haven't seen them either," Lynette said with a chuckle.

"Why not? Don't they still live at home?"

"You are out of the loop, Emmy. They started their second semester at Olivet last month."

"Get out!" Emmy shouted. "That can't be right."

"My pocketbook says otherwise. I can't imagine having two sets of twins like my friend Janae."

"The one who wrote that book, right?"

"Yes, Janae Wenger. She's written two more books about raising her twins. All four of her girls are going to Wheaton College."

"Oh, wow! That must cost a fortune," Emmy said.

"Tell me! Janae did say her books are paying for college though. How are your books selling? I read the one about Claire and Ruby when it came out. That was good."

Thanks, Lynette. The second one will be out soon. I'm not sure if I can let the girls read it yet."

"Sounds sinister."

Emmy laughed. "They are probably mature enough for the story, but maybe I'm not mature enough to handle their reactions."

"What? You not mature enough. How is that possible?" Lynette teased.

"How did Paul handle it when Ruth and Esther... you know?"

"Handle what?" Lynette asked with a straight voice.

"You know what I mean," Emmy said softly.

Lynette laughed hard enough to hurt her side. "You're still as immature as when I first met you. You can't even talk about it."

"I was just a baby when we met."

"You were, but you were in high school if I remember correctly. Anyway, Paul handled it like a mature adult male. He denied the possibility."

"Same with Kenny in a way. Saturday night he stubbed his toe and acted like the dork he is."

Twenty minutes later, Emmy said, "We really have to get together soon. It's terrible how life gets in the way at times."

"You could always stop by the church on Sunday morning, Emmy. We start at 10:45. Give or take."

Emmy snorted and said, "Nice try, but you know how that went the last time."

"Some of our older people are still rather resistant to any type of change. Especially when it comes to music. They insist we do as many hymns as contemporary songs. Paul gets frustrated with them, but what can he do."

"I thought your attendance was going up?"

"It has, but it's hit a plateau the last year or so. But that happens to most churches. Say hi to everyone for me."

"Definitely, and I will keep you and the older people in my prayers. Maybe one of these days they will realize all this preference stuff is not good for the church."

25

"Kenny, I'm going to the cemetery. I haven't been there for a while, and I should go," Emmy said Saturday morning.

He finished his coffee, pushed back his chair in the breakfast nook, and placed the cup in the sink. He faced Emmy and asked, "Would you like some company?"

She shook her head. "I'd rather go by myself."

Kenny looked at the calendar on the fridge. "Has it been a year already?"

"A year today. Some days it doesn't seem that long ago, but other times I feel she's been gone much longer. Weird, huh?"

He put his hands on her shoulders and kissed her cheek. "I haven't lost a parent, so I can't say I know how you feel. You've lost both of yours."

"I won't be gone long. Maybe we can do something together this afternoon," she said walking to the desk and grabbing her purse and then her keys from their place by the mudroom door.

Kenny grinned.

"I didn't mean that," she said.

Emmy turned into Rose Hill cemetery and drove slowly along the winding road until she came to the section where her relatives were buried. She parked, pulled her coat tighter around her and tried not to walk on grave markers. She stopped in front of her parents graves and closed her eyes. She prayed silently until she felt a hand on her shoulder.

"Shoot! Diane, you scared the crap out of me."

"Sorry, Em," Diane whispered. "I thought you heard me."

"How did you know I was here?"

"I called Kenny. He told me."

"Can you believe it's been a year?"

"And Daddy's been gone almost eleven years. Doesn't seem possible."

They moved to the gravesites of both sets of grandparents.

"It's funny, but I was thinking about Grandpa the other day," Emmy said.

"Which one?"

"Grandpa Colasanti. I never saw Grandpa Sandusky all that much. I was close to Grandma Isabel, but not him."

26

"He spent most of his time at work," Diane said letting the breeze blow her long brown hair around. "You should remember him taking us to the miniature golf place he owned."

"I remember going there, but he wasn't always with us. Didn't he own another business, too?"

"At one time or other, he owned several different businesses. Some of them made money, others didn't. But he left Grandma Isabel pretty well off."

"I'm so glad she made it to a hundred," Emmy said glancing at the Sandusky headstone.

Diane pulled her hair behind her head and grinned.

Emmy caught the grin and asked, "What's so funny? We're in a cemetery."

"I was looking at your hair. I don't remember a time when mine was this much longer than yours."

"I haven't let mine grow that long in several years. It's so much easier to take care of now." Emmy flipped her not-quite-shoulder-length hair around. "In fact, I need a trim."

"Are you going to make the girls cut their hair? Theirs is as long as yours was when you were thirteen, but it's not as frizzy."

"Mine's always been curly or wavy. It wasn't frizzy," Emmy insisted.

"If you say so, Em."

Emmy shrugged. "It's their choice. Isa has talked about it." Emmy stood still and sighed. "Crap! I forgot your birthday, didn't I? I'm so sorry."

Diane chuckled and said, "No big deal. You had a lot to handle last weekend. I'm glad I have three boys."

"It will be a long time before Lily has to go through it."

"How did Kenny handle it? I remember when we started. Daddy treated me like I was so fragile every time... you know."

"Did Daddy know when I started?"

Diane laughed. "Of course. By that time he was used to it."

"I didn't think he knew."

"He knew more about us than we thought."

"I hope not," Emmy whispered.

They paused by Heather Bertucci Khryzman's grave.

"What are you thinking, Em?"

"Dotty is fourteen and most people don't remember her birth mother. Everyone at church thinks of her and Peter as Tony and Sloane's kids."

"It's sad, but she can't remember Heather at all."

"I think of Heather a lot."

"Duh! You did name your first baby for her," Diane said.

"True, but I don't think of that all the time now. I used to think about it a lot more."

"It's getting windier. Can we go home now, please?" Diane asked.

They turned around and stopped in front of their parents' gravesite.

"Do you think they still argue and fight?" Emmy asked.

Diane snorted and said, "No doubt. But you always say heaven is like this perfect place where no one remembers the bad things."

"I like to think that's how it is, but we won't know until we're there, I guess." Emmy wrapped her arms over her chest as a gust of wind blew.

"Are you cold?"

"A little bit. Are you going to come back in February?"

Diane shook her head. "I don't think Daddy will mind if I came to see him a few weeks early. You?"

"Probably. I'm more sentimental than you."

Diane put an arm around Emmy's shoulders and squeezed. "That you are, little sister."

Chapter Three

Kenny entered the modern steel and glass building housing the Walker Management Group, took the elevator to the second floor and walked up to Mrs. Santos' desk.

"You aren't the last one here," Gladys Santos said while tapping a pencil in rhythm to the music emanating from Andy's office. She removed her glasses and pinched the bridge of her nose.

"He's jamming to some blues again, huh?" Kenny asked with a smile.

"I used to threaten to quit if he didn't turn it down, but he ignored me and gave me raises. Now I don't bother. He wants to meet in the conference room." She pointed down the hall. "I think he's finally gone deaf, though."

Kenny joined the rest of the guys, and five minutes later, Dave Persching arrived. Andy looked at his watch, but didn't say anything.

"Sorry I'm late, but I had to drop the kids off at school. Macy has to be at work at six on Tuesdays, and they missed the bus. At least I only had to drive to two different schools. Did I miss anything?"

"Not really," Kenny said. "We were just making small talk."

"Have you guys made a decision about the tour?" Andy asked. "I've been getting calls from promoters all across the country and the Prater-Saylor Agency needs an answer."

Kenny looked at P.J., who looked at Dave. Adam and Jeremy stared outside at the snow flurries.

"You guys are part of the team," Kenny said. "What do you want to do?"

"I talked to Jeff last night, and he said he would be pissed if we cancel the tour because of him," P.J. said.

"I would like to do another tour," Jeremy added. "Last fall was my first tour with the band in ages, and it felt great to be in front of crowds again."

After a brief discussion, it was agreed the summer Fridays

29

At Five tour would go on as planned.

"Now that we've settled that, we need to hire someone to play bass," Kenny said. "Any suggestions?"

"We could use Tommy," P.J. suggested.

Kenny shook his head. "Won't work. I asked Emmy if we could borrow him, and she said no way. It would be too much to ask him to play for both bands."

Adam raised a hand and said, "Do you remember Ryan Lederer? Stuart's son."

"Isn't he in a touring band?" Dave asked.

"He was, but they broke up. Jennifer decided she had enough of the road. She took a job as a worship pastor for a church in Knoxville."

"He's pretty good," Kenny said. "I don't know about his singing, but Adam can do all of Jeff's parts."

"I can call him and see if he's interested," Adam said. "The last I knew he was playing part-time with a local band and substitute teaching whenever he can."

"Sounds good," Andy said. "Unless there's something else, I have calls to make. It's not easy handling the career of Fridays At Five."

"I hate Mondays," Bobby O'Connor said plopping onto a couch in the control room of Kenny's basement recording studio. He twirled a drumstick in one hand and pointed at the mixing desk with the other stick. "That's new, right?"

Kenny spun around in his chair. "Yes, and this will be the second session I've used it. Do you want to know the details?"

"Not really, but I suppose you're going to tell me anyway."

"It's a custom API Trident Legacy with eighty inputs and the software is light-years ahead of what I had before." He explained technical details for three minutes and mentioned the price.

"Does Emmy know how much it cost?" Bobby asked standing up and leaning over the twelve foot wide console.

"No, and you better never tell her," Kenny warned.

Stuart Lederer and Bruce Sutherland entered the room.

30

They would be the recording engineers for these sessions. Stuart worked for Steward Music Group as a producer and engineer. He had worked with Fridays At Five on every project from the beginning. Bruce also worked for Steward Music, but handled the front-of-house duties for Emmy when she toured.

"Morning, guys," Bobby said standing up and twirling his sticks. "Do you guys know how to use this beast, or should I give you a lesson?"

"I might need a refresher, Bobby. How do you turn it on?" Stuart asked. He took a seat and faced Bobby.

"There's got to be a power switch somewhere." Bobby inspected the console, but then shrugged.

Bruce hit a switch on the wall to the right and the console and different banks of gear came to life in a choreographed sequence.

"Yeah, I knew that," Bobby said.

Within thirty minutes all the musicians had arrived and were in the large room where they actually played their instruments. Bobby O'Connor, who had been Emmy's drummer for the better part of fifteen years, was warming up in the drum booth. Adam Vicini and Isaac Ladlow checked the programs on their keyboards. Mason Williams ran his fingers up and down the frets of his bass guitar, and Boyd Goldman tuned the three guitars he would be using.

"Where is the princess?" Bobby asked.

"She will be here in a second," Kenny replied. "You know she's just doing scratch vocals today, right?"

Ten minutes later Emmy joined the guys, and they began to record what might be the title track of her final CD.

At dinner the following day Heather set her laptop on the breakfast nook table and showed it to Isabella.

"What am I supposed to see?" Isabella asked.

"This is Mom's page on Amazon."

"I can see that."

"Notice anything different?" Heather scrolled down the page.

"Wait! Go back. What is that?"

Heather scrolled back until Isabella hollered to stop.

"Is that the new book? What's the title?" Isabella asked.

That's Not Possible, Is It?" Heather answered. "It's book two in the Claire and Ruby series." Heather looked over her shoulder at her mother, who was draining some broccoli. "Mom! Why did it take so long to release this book? I thought you finished it at the end of last year."

"I needed to work on a couple chapters. Would someone help me? The garlic bread needs to come out of the oven, the spaghetti is done, and I need the olive oil for the broccoli."

The twins split the chores. Emmy pulled a bowl of salad from the refrigerator.

"Is dinner ready?" Kevin asked as he dashed out of the mudroom, slamming the door, and skating in his socks along the hardwood floor to the granite kitchen island. "I'm starving. Ben, Taylor, Caden and me were building a snow fort and the roof collapsed and buried Taylor, but we dug him out. Scout helped."

"What!? Is he okay? Where is he?" Emmy asked.

"He's fine. It was just a little bit, and it didn't cover his head," Kevin said.

"I'm so glad you rescued Taylor," Emmy said grabbing three different kinds of salad dressing from the fridge. "Dinner will be ready as soon as someone sets the table."

"I have to wash my hands," Kevin said disappearing into the powder room located next to the mudroom.

"I'll do it," Isabella said. "I don't mind setting the table, but Kevin or Heather has to clear the dirty dishes."

"Kenny! Dinner is ready," Emmy poked her head into the hallway and hollered five minutes later.

He emerged from the family room, and joined everyone in the breakfast nook.

"I noticed a layer of dust on the dining room table. When did we last use it?" he asked with a straight face.

"Two Sundays ago," Emmy answered. "We can use it every time we eat if you'd like, but you always insist we have an intimate dinner if it's just us. The table in there is too big for that."

"Maybe we should invite people over more often," Kenny suggested after praying.

"I can always invite Ben and Taylor," Kevin offered while grabbing two slices of garlic bread. "Zach and Caden, too."

Kenny asked the kids about school. They attended the Crest Ridge United Nazarene School which was affiliated with their church. The twins were in eighth grade, and Kevin was a sixth grader.

"Sorry, Daddy, but not much happened today," Isabella said. "No one got in trouble in any of our classes. We didn't have any pop quizzes, and lunch was the normal choices."

Kevin took a large bite of spaghetti and said, "Jarrett Bindley threw up his chocolate milk, and just missed nailing one of the teachers."

"Kevin Michael! Don't talk with your mouth full, and did you have to bring that up now?"

"Sorry, Mom, but that was the most exciting thing that happened today."

An hour later the dishes were done, the table cleaned and the leftovers put away.

"Do you have time to tell us about the book now, Mom?" Heather asked. "You only let us read a few chapters. What happens to Claire and Ruby this time?"

"I'm not sure I should tell you. This one might be a little mature for you and Isa," Emmy answered from her spot on the living room couch that faced the TV.

"Why?" Heather asked with a grin. "Is there a lot of sex in the book?"

"Heather Rose!" Emmy exclaimed.

Heather rolled her eyes. "Mom, we aren't babies. We know about sex. Tell us what happens or else I'll order one and read it without you knowing. I know how to use Amazon."

Emmy sighed and patted the couch next to her. "Okay, but don't tell your brother."

"Tell me what?" Kevin asked. He had just bounded down the stairs like a rhino in hot pursuit of a willing female.

"Nothing! Go away, Kevin," Heather yelled. "Isa and I are

33

talking to Mommy, and we don't need you around."

"Fine! I'm going downstairs."

Heather waited until Kevin was gone and asked, "What happens that is so naughty you don't want us to know?"

"You have to understand these characters are older than you and Isa," Emmy said.

"Yeah, we got that. They're in high school," Heather replied with a hint of sarcasm.

"Sometimes people don't always make the best choices," Emmy said and then took a deep breath. "Sometimes they do things they later regret, but once they've made a choice, they can't change it."

"Mom!" Heather dragged out the word. "Will you just tell us already?"

"The reason I felt undecided was because..." Emmy looked at both girls before continuing. "It's because Ruby makes a poor choice."

The girls waited, but Emmy didn't elaborate.

Heather stood up. "That's it. I'm ordering a copy. It will be here tomorrow."

"Fine! I'll tell you," Emmy said.

Heather sat back down with a smile.

"Ruby has sex with a boy," Emmy whispered.

"Whew! I thought you were going to say she was gay," Heather said.

"Did she really?" Isabella asked.

"She gave in to pressure to conform. She knew it wasn't the proper thing to do, but she did it anyway."

Emmy talked more about how Ruby and Claire responded differently to situations.

"Ruby could have said no and walked away, but she didn't."

"We know better than to cave in to peer pressure, Mom. We've talked about that in Sunday School and at regular school, too," Isabella added.

Heather tapped her cheek several times while staring at her mother. "There were several things that happened to Ruby in the first book that reminded me of stories you and Daddy have told us about when you were kids."

"Parts of the stories are based on real life. Why?" Emmy asked.

"Is the Ruby character really you, and is Claire really Aunt Diane?" Heather asked.

"Maybe in part," Emmy said.

Heather's eyes grew wide with surprise. "So you had sex when you were in high school."

"What? No!" Emmy waved both hands. "I did no such thing."

Isabella turned to face Emmy and Heather. "I think I see. You've kinda switch the characters. In real life Aunt Diane was more like Ruby even though Ruby is the younger sister. The Claire character is you because she does the right thing. She makes better choices. Am I right?"

"Partially, I suppose," Emmy said. "The characters are more like a combination of me and Diane and other people. I can see some of Annie O'Dell in Ruby. Not that Annie had sex..."

"Are you blushing, Mommy?" Isabella asked.

"Don't you have homework due tomorrow?" Emmy asked getting up and walking away.

Heather leaned close to Isabella and they high-fived.

"Hey, girls!" Emmy yelled as she headed down the hallway while staring at her cell phone.

"What?" Heather shouted back from her spot on the floor in front of the family room fireplace.

Isabella ran out of the family room and collided with Emmy. "Sorry, Mom. Why did you holler? We finished our homework at school. We are going to church tonight, right?"

"Yes, we're going. I'm supposed to help with the junior high kids tonight. I just got a text from Liz Hammond. Rebecca had the baby this afternoon," Emmy said.

"What did she have?" Isabella asked as they walked into the family room and sat on the couch. "You probably told me before, but I forgot."

"According to Liz, they had a boy. Seven pounds and seven ounces and..."

"What did they name him?" Heather asked without moving from her spot.

"Isaiah Joel," Emmy answered.

"I wondered why she hasn't been playing with the worship team," Isabella said.

"She took some time off because she had some issues."

"With the baby? Is he okay?"

"Liz said both of them are doing great. She is at Mercy Hospital with her."

"Why is she in Mercy?" Heather asked finally getting up. She sat next to her mother.

"I'm not sure, Heather. St. Bart's would be closer. I'll have to find out."

"If you go see her, can we go with?" Isabella asked.

"You might have to wait until she comes home to see the baby. Doctors are telling mothers to restrict who has contact with their babies a lot more than the old days."

"Like when we were born?" Heather asked. "I know we were early and had to stay in the hospital for like a month."

"It wasn't that long, but you were early. I don't think Rebecca's baby is early."

"Do you think Rebecca will come back to the worship team? I like how she plays the piano. She's a lot better than that lady who used to play. She played too loud."

"I'm pretty sure Rebecca will need time off to take care of Isaiah, but she will be back at some point. There's been talk about her joining the staff in a full-time position."

"Do you get paid for singing with the worship team?" Heather asked.

Emmy shook her head. "You know we don't get paid. Only the worship leader gets paid."

"Too bad. I was hoping to join the teen band and make some money," Heather said before heading upstairs. "Or you could raise my allowance."

Emmy's phone rang.

"Hi, Liz, are you still at the hospital? How are Rebecca and Isaiah doing?"

"I'm in the waiting area now. She was nursing him. They are both doing great. Isaiah has lots of dark hair, and I think he looks like Rebecca."

"You know it's too early to tell, right?"

"Yes, but I can see Rebecca in him. Ryan is still calling people. He comes from a large family."

"Why is she at Mercy instead of St. Bart's. Don't they live closer to St. Bart's?"

"They do, but her doctor works out of Mercy. Ryan grew up in New Linden, so Mercy is closer to his family."

"I didn't know that. I thought he was from SoHam."

"Tyler said he has ten baby dedications coming up. It's going to be part of the schedule every Sunday for a time."

"That's probably a good thing. It's one way of growing the church," Emmy joked. "I'll see you later. I have to study the lesson again. I don't see how you do it."

"Do what?" Liz asked.

"Well, you teach first grade at school. You teach a Bible class for the women twice a month. You take care of your kids and lots of other kids from the church. You teach on Wednesday night. You practice with the worship team on Thursdays..."

"I don't have to practice every week. We're on a rotation."

"I know. I don't think I could sing every week like I used to. You are always doing something. Don't you ever get to a point where you just want to crawl into bed and hibernate for a month?"

"I get tired like everyone, but every time I try to say no to something, God tells me I need to do it."

"We are so lucky to still have you and Tyler. I've always been afraid some other church would steal you guys from us."

"Tyler still says he wants to retire from here, but we have to listen to what God tells us."

"I know, but I hope he doesn't tell you to leave. In fact, I told him last night how much we need you to stay."

"You're a goof, Emmy," Liz said with a laugh. "But we love you anyway."

Chapter Four

"Mace Franklin! I haven't seen you in ages," Emmy said as she settled into her recliner in the den she now used more than Kenny. One leg sprawled across the arm and the other was tucked under her. "How are you. The last time I spoke to Annie, she said you were losing your hair and putting on a few pounds."

"It happens to all of us eventually. I thought you might make it to the class reunion, but I suppose you have a rather hectic schedule. What with maintaining a career as a singer and now a famous author."

"Oh, hush. My career as a mother of teenagers makes my life hectic as you put it. How is your career going? You are still teaching, right?"

Mace leaned back in his chair and nodded as his secretary dropped three student files on his desk and walked away. He glanced out the window and watched two security guards pacing the sidewalk.

Emmy continued, "Why would I attend your class reunion? You were a year ahead of me. Was Annie there? She graduated a year early just to start college with all her friends."

Mace planted his feet on the floor and picked up one of the files. He glanced at the name Hodges and chuckled. "I thought you graduated early, too. Am I incorrect?"

"I did, but only one semester early."

"Right," he said opening the file. "Annie said you graduated early, and I assumed incorrectly."

"It doesn't seem possible we've been out of high school long enough to have a reunion already," Emmy said shifting to a more comfortable position.

"Twenty plus years goes by in a flash," Mace said.

"How's the basketball team doing? You are still coaching, aren't you?"

"I am still coaching the varsity, but I'm also the vice-principal now," he answered.

"Get out! Did Mr. Kemmerick finally retire?"

Mace coughed once. "Actually, he passed away in 2014."

"Oh, I'm sorry. I didn't know. I am so out of the loop, as I was reminded recently. Had he been sick?"

"No, not really. He suffered a heart attack at home. It's a shame. He retired and two months later was gone." Mace snapped his fingers. "With all the budget cuts and the state funding not being what it used to, I'm taking on two roles. In a way, I like it. Coaching basketball is my passion, but being vice-principal pays better. At least in high school."

"I remember the year Roosevelt won the basketball championship down in Peoria. You were the star of the team."

"It was a team effort, Emmy."

"Yeah, yeah. You have to say that, but we both know you were the reason the team won."

"I'm calling because I have a slight connection to you, and one of the student after-school activity clubs has made a request."

"We have more than a slight connection. Annie is a mutual friend even if we don't socialize as much as we should."

"I'll get right to the point. The Aspiring Writers of America club would like to invite you to speak at one of their meetings before the end of the school year. I know you are busy..."

"They want me?" Emmy asked incredulously. "Why?"

Mace stared at his cell phone. "Seriously?"

"Okay, I've written some stuff, but I'm not a famous writer. They should ask my editor. Denise Bartell is famous for real."

"She has spoken to the group several times over the years. I think they would like to hear from someone... younger, perhaps."

"I'm not that young anymore," Emmy said thinking about how much her girls were changing.

"You are closer to their age than Ms. Bartell and some of the other speakers they've invited."

"Did they have a certain time in mind?"

Mace looked at his memo. "It's probably too late for you to schedule something in March. Would you be free sometime in April or May?"

"I could probably free up the time, but I'm not sure I could talk to a bunch of high school writers. They probably know more about writing than me."

Mace chuckled and said, "I'm sure they think they do, but in reality, they don't know enough to know... A little knowledge is a dangerous thing is what I'm trying to say."

"Do you need an answer right now?"

"No, take all the time you need to decide. You can call me at this number or call the school."

"I'll think about it, and call you back in a day or two. It was nice to hear from you, Vice-Principal Franklin," Emmy said and then giggled.

Mace laughed and leaned back in his chair. He intertwined his fingers behind his neck to relieve the stress and tried to remember the last time he saw Emmy in person. He leaned forward again and called out, "Mrs. McClurg, please send Brad Hodges in now."

"Who were you talking to?" Kenny asked poking his head into the room.

"Mace Franklin," Emmy said and then told Kenny the details.

"So, the Vice-Principal of Theodore Roosevelt is calling you. Are you in trouble? Did he give you another detention?"

"I never had to go to detention," Emmy insisted though she really couldn't remember.

"You should do it. You know more than a fifth-grader about how to write."

"Doubtful, but these are high school students. I should know more than them."

"If no one has anything else to add, I'll pray and end our staff meeting," Senior Pastor Tyler Hammond said Monday morning. Still only thirty-four years of age, Tyler had been senior pastor of Crest Ridge United Nazarene since November of 2011. He prayed to close the meeting and gathered his notes.

"Do you have a few minutes to talk?" Wyatt Pearson, Tyler's chief associate pastor, asked after everyone else left. "Shouldn't take long."

"I was going to grab lunch at Darby's because I need to run up to St. Bart's. Care to join me?"

"How can I pass up a trip to Darby's Dogs? And to the hospital. Love going there."

"Everyone in SoHam calls it Darby's. You will sound like a tourist if you add the dogs."

"Good to know. I'll grab my coat and wallet."

Tyler chuckled because his college friend, roommate and best man at his wedding had a reputation for being frugal.

"You don't have to go to St. Bart's with me." Tyler said thinking about Wyatt's late wife Evie, who passed away from breast cancer. "We can talk here. I won't starve."

"I do have a craving for one of their chili cheese dogs. I can help with the hospital visits, Tyler. Evie has been gone over five years. I still miss her, but life goes on."

"I'll grab my coat and meet you in the foyer. I promised Liz I would check on David. He was coughing this morning."

"It's a good thing the church has a daycare with a nurse to help run it," Wyatt replied. "Meet you out front."

Because of traffic, it took over thirty minutes to go from Crest Ridge to the one-of-a-kind, locally-owned hot dog stand located close to the Kinmundy River in the South Hampshire neighborhood of Raynor Park.

"The street where Kenny Colwell and Emmy grew up is close, isn't it?" Wyatt asked as they got out of Tyler's Prius.

Tyler pointed. "That's Ruby and this is Campbell. If you take Campbell to East Fifth Street and turn right, it's up a couple blocks. If I have my geography right. Might be three blocks."

Wyatt held the door open and they waited in line to order their food.

"I'll bring that right out, Pastor Tyler," the young man behind the counter said with a smile.

"Thanks. We'll be over there somewhere," Tyler said. He and Wyatt filled their cups and found a booth. "There are so many kids in the youth group now. I can remember most of them, but I don't remember that guy's name," Tyler said.

"Daryl introduced me to him last Sunday. His name is... I can't think of it right now, but it was not a common name. I'll probably think of it later."

41

The tall, husky young man brought out their order a few minutes later.

"Can I get you anything else?" he asked.

"We're good for now," Tyler said. "Would you join us in prayer, or do you have to get back to work?"

The young man glanced over his shoulder at the line waiting to order. "I don't have much time."

"I'll make it quick," Tyler said with a chuckle. He quickly prayed for the meal and the young man who delivered it.

"Thanks, Pastor Tyler. I gotta get back," he said hooking a thumb over his shoulder.

"Talk to you later," Tyler said.

Wyatt dumped his fries onto his tray and grabbed the ketchup bottle. Tyler watched as Wyatt covered the fries with enough ketchup to fill a soup bowl.

"What?" Wyatt asked looking up.

"Care for some fries with... never mind. I've seen Emmy do the same thing." Tyler added some salt to his fries. "What did you want to talk about?"

"I would like your opinion concerning my dating a certain person."

"So, it's true. You are seeing Kristen Randolph, huh?"

"A few times. I really like her. I feel comfortable with her."

Tyler stared at Wyatt.

"Maybe comfortable is the wrong word. I haven't felt close to anyone since Evie passed. I keep my distance and don't let anyone get close. I feel different about Kristen."

"She is very nice," Tyler said. "She has been part of the church almost as long as Emmy and Kenny."

"Do you have any concerns about her marital situation?"

Tyler took the last bite of his dog before answering, "Years ago I don't think people would accept a minister dating someone who was divorced."

"Does it matter that I..." Wyatt paused and glanced around the busy restaurant. "I saw Kristen at church my first Sunday and felt an attraction of some sort. Don't ask me why, but I felt something. I didn't know her name or anything about her. I think it was her smile that caught my eye."

"I can understand your attraction."

"I am fully aware of what our church manual says about divorce. Marriage has always been an until death vow for me. Kristen's divorce was the result of her husband's infidelity. I've been told she did her best to repair the brokenness, but her husband did not value the marriage as he should have. I would like to know I have your approval if I move forward in this relationship. I don't need an answer right now, but as soon as you know, would you tell me, please?"

Tyler nodded. "After Liz told me you were seeing Kristen, I prayed about this, and I can tell you now. Given the circumstances in this situation, I can approve your decision to... explore a deeper relationship with her. As your friend, I hope you find someone, not to replace Evie, but to share the rest of your life."

"As my pastor?" Wyatt asked.

"I won't fire you if something develops between you and Kristen."

Wyatt took a deep breath then sighed.

Several minutes later immediately after Tyler took a large bite of his second chili cheese dog, Wyatt said, "Fez."

Tyler tried not to choke as he asked, "What?"

"Fez! That's his name. Or it's what he goes by. His real name is Antonio or Anthony." Wyatt scratched his ear. "Anthony. Anthony Rivera. See! I knew I'd remember his name given enough time."

"It's good to know you aren't losing your mind," Tyler teased. "Is he from SoHam?"

"If I remember correctly, Pastor Wiley said he has no family here and grew up somewhere in Wisconsin. Oh, I remember now," Wyatt said waving a fry around. "Do you remember the TV show called *That '70s Show*?"

"I remember it, but I doubt if I ever watched it. Why?"

"There was a character in the show that got picked on..." Wyatt explained much more than necessary about the plot of the show.

43

"So, Fez grew up as the only Mexican in a small Wisconsin city." Tyler grabbed his last two fries.

"To the best of my knowledge, that is why people call him Fez. Though, I think he spells it with an S not a Z."

"You are always very thorough, Wyatt. Ready to have some fun?"

"Yeah, St. Bart's is calling. I'll take the trays back."

Wyatt placed the trays on the counter and looked for Fez but didn't see him.

"Ready?" Tyler asked.

"How many people are in the hospital?"

"Four, unless Jim Rosek went home. He was complaining about his heart, so Stella took him to the ER last night."

"He's a tough ol' guy. He'll probably outlive both of us," Wyatt said as they left.

"Do you have plans for tonight, Krissy? If you don't maybe we could get together and read cookbooks or something," Emmy said trying not to laugh.

Kristen shook her head at her cell phone. "You know perfectly well Wyatt is taking me to dinner, Emily. Don't pretend you don't know."

"I'm only calling because the girls insisted. What are you gonna wear? Did you buy a dozen new dresses for the occasion?"

"Those days are long gone. I picked out three from my closet and have been trying to decide which one I like best."

"Ask Gracie. She can tell you which one looks the best," Emmy said shaking her head at the twins and waving for them to go away. "Has she said anything more about you and Wyatt?"

"She told me it was all right if Pastor Wyatt and I go on dates."

"And Zach?"

"He refuses to talk about it. He thinks his father will leave his new wife and come back."

"That's not gonna happen," Emmy said.

"Gee, thanks."

"Oh, I didn't mean it like that. If he had a brain, he would."

"I actually asked Tony to talk to him. He said he would, but he suggested maybe Peter try first. Zach and Peter have always been close despite the difference in age."

"They're only two and a half years apart," Emmy said. "That's the same as me and Diane."

"Great example! You and your sister have always been best friends."

"Okay, don't be so sarcastic. Maybe I should have chosen a better example," Emmy admitted. "Call me later and tell me about dinner."

"It's just dinner, Em."

"I can always hope. Later."

"Zach, Peter is coming over to hang out while I go to dinner," Kristen said just after five.

Zach set his iPad down and looked at her. "Are you going out with that guy from church again?"

"Yes, and his name is Wyatt. You can be polite at least if you talk to him."

"I'll stay in my room. That way we don't have to talk to each other."

Grace walked up to her older brother. "Why are you being such a jerk? Pastor Wyatt is really nice. He likes Mommy and treats her better than Daddy did."

"No he doesn't! I don't care what anyone says." Zach stomped up the stairs, slammed his bedroom door hard enough to rattle the pictures on the wall and locked it.

Peter arrived five minutes later, and after talking to his aunt Kristen, he headed upstairs to Zach's room and knocked.

"I'm not coming out, Mom!" Zach hollered.

"Hey, Zach, it's Peter. Can I talk to you?"

Zach opened the door but blocked the way in. "Hi, Peter. Did you hear about Mom going out again with that guy from church?"

"Yeah, I know." Peter looked into the room and saw Zach's cherished Starfighter IV model on his bed. "Have you been waging war against the evil empire again?"

"I was, but just because I'm mad at Mom." Zach moved to

45

his bed and sat down. "She should be with Dad."

"You shouldn't be mad at your mother. It's not her fault your Dad lost his mind and moved out."

"He didn't lose his mind!"

Peter spun Zach's desk chair around. "Are you sure about that? Don't you think your mom is pretty special?"

"She's the best mom anyone could have."

Peter shrugged and asked, "Would it make sense to leave her?"

Zach held his model and inspected it for a moment before answering, "I guess not, but that doesn't mean Dad is crazy."

"He's probably not crazy, but everyone thinks he made a really bad decision. You know why?"

"No, why?"

"He lost his focus on God. He allowed sin to enter his life and become overpowering. It clouded his judgment and he lost his way."

"He used to go to church all the time, but he kinda stopped. He would get mad at Mom because she always goes to church and takes me and Gracie."

"I haven't known Pastor Wyatt very long, but he's pretty cool. He talks to the teens and listens even though he's not the youth pastor."

"That's Pastor Wiley. He's okay, and his wife is nice to us. Some of the high school boys were making fun of my models, and she made them stop and apologize."

"I still think all your models are cool, Zach. You know so much about the Starfighter world. More than anyone I know."

"I have all the books, too." Zach pointed to his floor-to-ceiling bookcase.

"Did anyone ever tell you about Pastor Wyatt's wife?"

"Someone said she's dead."

Peter nodded. "That's true. Her name was Evie and she and Pastor Wyatt got married after college. They loved each other very much. But then she got cancer. She fought hard, but it was too much and she died. Pastor Tyler and Pastor Wyatt are like best friends, and he told us the story. It made him really sad when his wife died, and it's taken a long time to get over it. Papa told me that your mom is the only lady Pastor Wyatt has talked to very much in five years. You know how God sometimes tells adults what to do?"

"Yeah, Mom said it's the Holy Spirit." Zach set his model on the dresser and faced Peter. "Do you think the Holy Spirit is telling Mom and Pastor Wyatt to be friends?"

Peter nodded. "I think so. They will start out as friends, and if something happens, they might become more than friends. Adults fall in love sometimes and we can't understand why. Look at Papa and Mom. Uncle Kenny and Aunt Emmy grew up almost next door to each other. They were friends for a long time and then fell in love."

"Mom always says Aunt Emmy is like the most loving person she knows."

"Look, Zach. All I'm saying is that you need to pray about how you feel about this guy and cut him some slack. I read somewhere in The Bible that the rulers in Jerusalem were all hot and bothered because Jesus was teaching stuff. They wanted to … you know... kill him. But there was this one guy with one of those weird names. I forget what it was. Anyway, he told these other ruler guys that if Jesus wasn't like God, it wouldn't last, but if He was God, there wasn't anything they could do to stop it. You get my drift?"

"You're telling me if God wants Mom and Wyatt to be together, there's nothing I can do to stop it."

"And if they're not supposed to be together, they will find out pretty quick."

"And there's nothing I can do about it, huh?"

"Well, you can continue to be a snot and make everyone mad, but that's not helping anyone."

Zach thought for a moment. "Okay, I get it. I'll try not to be such a jerk. If he makes Mom happy, I should be happy, too."

Peter slapped Zach's back. "There's a pizza in the oven. Will you split it with me?"

"Sure. What about Gracie?"

"She can have part of my share."

47

The doorbell rang at 6:02.

"That's probably Pastor Wyatt," Zach said jumping up from his kitchen chair. "I'll let him in."

He opened the door and smiled.

"Good evening, Zachary. How are you? Is your mom ready for dinner?"

"Come in, Pastor Wyatt. She's still deciding what to wear, but she should be ready in a couple minutes. I'll let her know you're here."

"Thank you, Zachary. Oh, should I call you Zachary or do you prefer Zach?"

"Only my teachers call me Zachary. I'll let Mom know." He turned around and hollered up the stairs, "Mom! Pastor Wyatt is here. He's ready to go eat."

Wyatt grinned. He looked up the stairs and his grin turned into a full smile as Kristen descended.

"I hope I didn't keep you waiting too long."

"He just got here, Mom. I let him in," Zach said. He looked at the dress his mother wore. "Wow! You look pretty good. I'll have to tell Aunt Emmy you decided to wear a fancy dress. She said she would have worn old bluejeans."

"That sounds like Aunt Emmy," Peter said. "Papa used to tease her about being a tomboy when they were kids."

Wyatt offered his arm. "Shall we go?"

Zach and Grace watched their mother leave.

"Have fun and bring home the leftovers," Zach hollered before closing the door.

Chapter Five

"Good afternoon, Ryan. It's Kenny Colwell."

"Howdy to you, and how's the family?" Ryan Lederer asked.

"They're all good. How was church today?"

"We had a good service and a larger than normal turnout."

"Does Jennifer like being a worship leader? Emmy enjoys being a part of the team, but she doesn't want to have the responsibility of leading it."

"Our church isn't all that big, so she leads the singing with a small band. She really likes not having to travel," Ryan said with a laugh.

"Have you had a chance to talk to her about our offer?"

"Yes I have."

Kenny could hear the drawl in Ryan's voice though he had been born and raised in SoHam. He moved to Knoxville, Tennessee, after marrying Jennifer Sinclaire.

"We are hoping your answer will be yes."

Ryan laughed, turned to look at his wife, who was still eating lunch, and said, "How could I refuse such a generous offer? The alternative would be playing in a local country band making fifty bucks a night on the weekends."

"Great! I'll let Andy know, and he can have the contract sent to you. It's pretty simple, but you can have someone look at it if you want. Basically, you are hired for the duration of the tour and get paid whatever it was you and Andy agreed on every week. You receive a stipend, or per diem, I don't remember which is the proper term. Lunch money kinda."

"The offer was very generous. I'm not sure if you guys have always paid your touring musicians that much, but it's more than I've ever made. Thanks, and Jennifer thanks you, too."

"You are welcome. We will start rehearsing in mid May. We will put you up in a hotel until the tour starts."

"I appreciate that, but I was going to stay with Mom and Dad. They have plenty of room since all us kids have moved out."

"Let us know if you need a hotel. Andy's office will take

49

care of your flight into SoHam and home again after it's done. Any questions?"

"I know you guys change the set list up a bit every night. Do you have a master list you work from?"

"Yeah, we have a huge dart board."

Ryan laughed. "Emmy used to tease us about that. She claimed you guys would confuse the tech guys just to have fun."

"We used to mess with their minds, but with all the technology now, they have the settings for every song we do stored in the computers. All it takes is a split-second to load them up and they're good. Sometimes I see them laughing at us."

"I've been practicing the songs I know you do about every night."

"Ryan, we have faith in your ability to play. Don't feel like you have to imitate Jeff. Be yourself. Just make sure you can sing the harmony."

"What! I have to sing?" Ryan's deep voice raised in pitch.

"Just kidding. Adam does Jeff's part most of the time even when Jeff's playing. You can sing if you want, but it's not part of the job description."

"Good to know. Jennifer says I sound like a opossum cornered up a tree when I sing in the shower."

"I'm grateful the hospital arranged for this hotel, but it would have been so much more convenient had the closing on the house not been delayed," Rochelle Porter said while sipping her coffee Monday morning.

Rory Porter opened the box of pastries, selected one with what appeared to be cherry filling and sat beside her. "That's the only thing that's gone wrong with this move back to SoHam."

"Are you sure no one knows we've moved back?"

He shook his head. "We did tell Father James."

Rochelle drained her coffee and said, "I meant beside him. He hasn't told Emmy or Kenny or anyone, right?"

"Not a chance! He thinks this is worth the surprise. He's going to meet me in front of her parents' old house at three. He's going to FaceTime her and I'm going to walk up behind him.

50

Kinda in and out of the picture until she catches on or asks who keeps... is it photo bombing... I think so. Anyway, she's bound to see it's me sooner or later. Then I'll tell her I just happened to go for a long walk and ended up in SoHam."

"I give the whole thing a ten percent chance of working." She looked at the clock. "We need to go. Our first shift at Mercy Hospital awaits."

"Sorry I'm a few minutes late," Emmy said sounding out of breath that afternoon. "We were trying to finish this new track, and Kenny couldn't get the bass line right. I had to hum it to him the way I heard it. What's up? Why did you want to FaceTime at exactly three?" she asked then paused. "I didn't know you even knew how to FaceTime."

"Isabella showed me how, and I'm using her old iPad." He walked a few feet to get out from under a tree and faced the street.

"Where are you? It looks like you're outside."

"I am. I thought I would go for a walk since it's such a warm afternoon."

"Maybe in Florida or Arizona," she said with a laugh. "It's just above freezing here. We might get snow later tonight." She saw something in the background that looked familiar. "Hang on!"

"What?"

"Turn a bit to the right and hold the iPad out a little."

"Like this?" he asked.

"Yeah! Is that our old house?" she asked looking closely. "It is. What on earth are you doing there? Hey! Did someone just walk past you?"

"Huh? I didn't see anyone," he lied.

"There's someone there. I can see a shadow."

Rory chose that moment to walk past Father James again.

"What's going on? There is someone with you. Who?"

Father James turned in a circle. "I don't know what you're talking about." He took a step back off of the sidewalk and turned the iPad to give Emmy an unobstructed view of the old house. Rory stepped in front of the iPad but with his back to it."

"Dear brother, I know your eyesight is pathetic, but can you see the person standing almost right in front of you?"

51

"Oh, that guy?"

"Uh, yeah, he would be the one," Emmy said.

"Oh, he was walking up the sidewalk and stopped to look at the house. Why?"

Emmy sighed and shook her head. "I don't know what you're doing, but if you don't get out of the cold, you're going to freeze what few brain cells you have left. Tell whoever that is to either say something, get out of the way, or... I don't know."

"Excuse me, dear fellow," Father James said in the worst English accent ever. "Would you mind saying a few words to my dear younger sister?"

As the man turned around, Father James lowered the iPad so Emmy couldn't see above the man's shoulders.

"What should I say?"

"Tell him to talk louder," Emmy said.

The man cleared his throat. "Testing one, two. Check one. Check two."

Emmy stared as Father James slowly lifted the iPad.

"Rory Porter! What the..."

"Language, young lady," Father James warned while shaking a finger and jiggling the image.

"Is this some technology trick Barry Newton taught you? He's always been a geek."

"It's not a trick."

"Rory Clarence Porter, what on earth are you doing in SoHam, and why are standing in front of my old house?"

"I believe this house belonged to your parents, and how are you, Em?" he asked with a stupid-looking grin.

"Why are you here?" Emmy asked with the sternest face she could muster. "Mickel Boyanov, unless you want to be excommunicated by the pope, you will immediately tell me why Rory is here. There. With you, whatever."

"Maybe if we go for a little walk, I can explain," Rory said.

Rory and Father James headed west, along the sidewalk once familiar to Emmy and Rory.

"Keep the iPad steady."

"I am trying," Father James said.

"Let me hold it. I can talk to Emmy until we get where we're going." Rory took the iPad, grinned at her and asked, "How have you been? We haven't seen you since the accident."

"We? Is Rochelle with you?"

"Not at the moment, but she is in SoHam."

"I am fine..."

Rory stopped in front of two-story house that obviously needed some tender loving care. He pointed the iPad at the house while Emmy kept talking.

"Wait! Is that your old house? The one where you used to live when we were kids?"

"Sorta, but not exactly," he answered.

"Yes it is! That's where you lived. It belonged to your grandparents, right?"

"It did at one time, but now it belongs to me and Rochelle."

"No it doesn't," she said.

He turned the iPad back on himself and nodded. "Actually, it will belong to us on the twenty-first. It would have been ours last Friday, but there was an issue with the title company."

Emmy bit her lip and stared at Rory.

Father James stepped into the picture. "I think Rory is telling you that he and Rochelle bought the house."

"Why? They live in Florida."

"That's not technically true anymore."

"Explain!" she ordered.

"Okay, a while back Rochelle and I discussed the possibility of moving back to SoHam. We decided to do it, and we both got jobs at Mercy Hospital. Today was our first day actually."

"Go on."

"We needed a house to live in, and this one was for sale..."

"It's a dump! Why would you buy it? Are you planning to knock it down and build a new house?"

"No, we plan to renovate it." Rory waved a hand to include the whole street. "This part of Raynor Park is changing. Young couples are buying these old houses and fixing them up."

"So you're buying it as an investment, huh?"

"Maybe, but we're going to live here. It's fairly close to

53

work, and the house may not look like much on the outside, but it has good bones."

"Yeah, and those bones are probably buried in the basement. You should talk to Jeff and Frances if you need advice on renovations. They've done six or seven places in Timberline Heights."

Kenny walked by at that moment and Emmy grabbed his arm. "Look who I'm talking to."

He looked. "Hey, Rory. How's life in Florida?"

"Kenny, look closer."

He watched as Rory panned the iPad in a circle. "What am I supposed to see? Wait! That kinda looks like East Fifth Street, but that's not possible."

"I'm afraid it is, Kenny." Rory pointed the camera at the house. "Remember this place?"

"Sure. That's your old house. Looks rather rundown."

"He and Rochelle just bought it," Emmy said.

"Why?" Kenny asked.

Rory explained.

"Cool! Welcome back to SoHam. You guys have to come over. The kids will go nuts when they hear Uncle Rory is back."

They talked for several minutes.

"Then it's decided. You guys are coming for dinner tomorrow night. I'll order your favorite from Kerry Lynn's Pizza and Pasta."

"It's still in business, huh?" Rory asked.

"And so is Darby's, but you must know that since you are so close."

"Shoot! Good thing you mentioned Darby's. I'm supposed to stop and bring dinner home."

"We will see you tomorrow night. Now I want to talk to my brother," she insisted.

"Ooops! I think you might be in trouble," Rory said handing the iPad to Father James.

"Yes, my precious little sister whom I love dearly."

"Cut the crap! You knew about this and didn't tell me. You are in such trouble you're going to be in purgatory for a lifetime."

"Does that mean I can't come over for dinner tomorrow?"

"You better come so I can yell at you in person," she said. "Maybe I won't hate you as much by then."

"When is Uncle Rory going to get here?" Kevin asked again.

Emmy pointed to the kitchen clock. "I told you they would be here around six. Do you know what time it is now?"

"It's 5:47," he answered. "Aw, Mom, I know how to tell time even on an old-fashioned clock."

"Will you wait in the garage for the pizza, please? It's already paid for, but the driver needs a tip. Give him this." She pulled a ten dollar bill from her purse and handed it to her son. "Don't forget and leave the service door open for Rory."

He grabbed the bill with a grin and said, "Ten bucks just for driving around delivering pizza. What a cool job. That's what I'm going to do in high school."

Five minutes after the pizza arrived Father James, Rory and Rochelle knocked on the mudroom door and came on in.

"Is anyone home?" Rory asked.

A small stampede thundered toward the kitchen from different parts of the house.

"Why didn't you tell us you were moving back?" Kevin asked while hugging Rory.

The girls surrounded Rochelle and peppered her with questions.

Emmy came to the rescue. "Girls, you can ask all your questions while we eat."

"We're eating in the dining room tonight," Kevin said. "Mom spent an hour cleaning it this afternoon."

"I dusted it," Emmy explained. "We haven't used it for a while."

"I smell pizza," Father James said as he headed to the dining room.

Everyone took a seat and Emmy prayed.

"Are you going to take care of babies at the hospital?" Heather asked before Rochelle could take a bite.

55

"Maybe we should hold off on the cross-examination until after dinner," Kenny suggested with a look that said to do otherwise would not be met with approval.

"Does anyone want the last piece?" Emmy asked later.

"I'll take it so you won't have leftovers," Rory said.

"Can we talk to Rochelle now?" Heather asked.

"I'm sure she doesn't want to be pestered," Kenny answered.

Rochelle waved a hand. "It's all right. We can sit in the family room and get caught up on the latest news."

The ladies headed to the family room, and the guys used the breakfast nook to talk.

"Is it hard to be a real nurse?" Heather asked. "I have a friend at school whose mom is a nurse. She helps deliver babies. I think that would be the perfect job. You get to take care of lots of babies."

"Some hospitals require the nurses to work twelve hour days. Those can be exhausting. Mercy still schedules eight hour shifts, but the downside to that is I have to work five days a week."

"Do you and Uncle Rory drive to work together?" Isabella asked.

"Some weeks we will be able to, but for right now, my hours will fluctuate weekly."

While the 'women' were talking about working in a hospital and taking care of babies, the 'men' used the breakfast nook to talk about renovating the old house.

"Is there really a big room in the attic?" Kevin asked.

Rory nodded.

"There is a huge space in our attic," Kenny said. "It's full of rafters and support beams though. You couldn't make it into one giant room."

"That sucks," Kevin sighed. "I need a bigger room."

"Or perhaps fewer possessions," Father James suggested.

An hour later Rory and Rochelle said goodbye for the night and left for the hotel.

"I think I might be a nurse when I grow up," Isabella said. "I like to take care of people."

"It's not an easy job," Emmy said.

"Miss Genna at church takes care of babies. I would want to do that, but I know old people need nurses, too."

"That's gross!" Heather said. "You have to change their diapers and give them baths. That would make me want to puke."

"I'd rather take care of babies," Isabella admitted.

"What would you like to be, Heather?" Emmy asked.

"I have no clue, but no way do I want to be a nurse. They have to spend too much time going to college."

Emmy grinned and said, "Fortunately, you have plenty of time to decide. I didn't know what I wanted to do until I was already married and had three wonderful children."

"But you worked for Grandpa Robertson. Didn't you like doing that?" Isabella asked.

"I did, and it was the perfect job for me at the time. Mr. Robertson was the best boss in the world."

"Oh, Mom," Isabella said giving her mother a hug.

"Yeah, we know you wanted to marry Daddy," Heather added.

"I did want to do that," Emmy agreed. "Tomorrow is a school day. It's time for bed."

Heather turned to Isabella. "I can't wait to be old enough not to have a curfew."

"I wish I had a curfew," Emmy whispered.

"Liz, what's wrong? You sound upset," Emmy said as Liz called later than normal.

"Larry just called me. He said they have to do an emergency C-section on Allie because Maggie is in distress."

Emmy gasped and fought back tears. "I'm so sorry, Liz. I'll start praying for them right now."

"Thank you, Emmy. Larry's at the hospital now, and I will keep you informed."

"They moved to Tennessee somewhere, right?"

"Yes, they live outside of Jackson City, and that's where the hospital is."

Emmy told Kenny and the kids right away, and they prayed

together for baby Maggie.

Thirty or so minutes later Emmy saw a message on her phone from Liz.

"Maggie is here!"

"What?" Kenny asked.

"Where?" the girls asked together.

"Liz just sent a picture and a message. Both the baby and her mother are doing okay. Wow! Maggie weighed over ten pounds."

"She's half grown," Kenny said. "I'm glad they're okay. I need to go to bed."

Emmy received another message from Liz early the next morning. She poked Kenny's side to wake him up.

"What, Em? It's still dark outside."

"Liz texted. Maggie is having trouble breathing and is in Intensive Care. We have to keep praying for Maggie and Allie," Emmy said.

"I'll pray for Larry, too. I'm sure he's worried sick."

Maggie kept improving every day and was released from the hospital on March 19.

"She's so cute," Emmy said as she walked down the hallway holding her laptop.

"Who's cute?" Kenny asked as he made a tuna sandwich.

"Maggie Kimmerle. Liz sent some photos. She was released from the hospital this morning. She wants to thank everyone for their prayers."

"Maggie?"

"No, you goof. Liz! She thanks everyone who prayed for Maggie and her parents. Allie is doing great, and Maggie is even nursing."

"TMI, Em. The nursing part, I mean."

Chapter Six

Nine days later Rory texted Emmy. "We have the keys to the house." He didn't expect an immediate reply, but his phone chirped a few minutes later. He read the text and chuckled.

"Was that Emmy?" Rochelle asked.

"Of course. She wants to know when she and Kenny can stop by the house. What should I tell her?"

"Tell her to come after four. We can show them the house and eat at Darby's."

"We can't eat at Darby's every day, Rochelle."

"I know. I would gain a hundred pounds, but we don't have anything in the house. We won't have any furniture until next Wednesday. Did you line up someone to be here for the movers?"

"Father James agreed to meet them here. St. John's is pretty close, and he said he could make time."

"Has the house changed much since you lived here?" Rochelle asked as she and Rory walked through the kitchen. She ran a hand over the laminated countertop.

"The rooms are still the same. This has always been the kitchen. Everything has been painted, and this ugly carpeting wasn't here." He gagged at the sight of the hideous green carpeting in the hallway and small family room.

"We can rip it out before the furniture arrives. Do you know what's underneath?"

"There's a hardwood floor in every room except the kitchen and bathroom on this floor. The hallway upstairs is hardwood, but I can't remember if the bedrooms have it. They were always carpeted when we lived here."

"Was the attic always one giant room?"

"Yeah, Owen used it as his private domain when he got to high school," Rory said. He looked at the stairs and thought about the years he lived in the house.

"How long ago did you move out?" Rochelle asked putting her hand on his shoulder.

"It was late September of 1996. I've told you the reason I left, right?"

"Yes, and Emmy told me how hurt she was because you never said goodbye."

"It was for the best." Rory climbed the stairs holding Rochelle's hand. At the top of the stairs he turned left and they stood in the doorway of a bedroom. "This was Amy's room."

Rochelle rubbed his back without speaking.

Rory turned around. "This was Mom's room most of the time, but as we got older, she used that small room at the back of the house."

"Which one was yours?" Rory moved past the door leading to the attic and opened the door at the end of the hallway. "This was mine."

"It's pretty small," Rochelle said stepping into the room and looking around.

"It was big enough."

"Did Emmy spend much time over here with Amy?"

"Off and on, I guess. Emmy was a couple years older than Amy, but Amy was more mature if you know what I mean. Emmy was naive about certain things. She was a tomboy until maybe her last year of high school."

"She wasn't interested in boys, huh?" Rochelle asked with a gleam in her eyes. "Not even a certain boy who lived down the street?"

"She and Kenny were close, but they were like brother and sister in many ways."

"I didn't mean him."

Rory looked out the window. "She and Barry Newton were friends but nothing more. He was one of those geeks before there was such a thing. He was terrible at sports, so Emmy didn't like him as more than a friend."

"You told me you liked to play football when you were younger. Did Emmy play with you and your friends?"

"She liked to play football with all the kids. There weren't many kids her age along Fifth Street. She hung out with older kids. Diane's friends at times. My friends on occasion. My friends weren't into sports like she was."

"She tutored you for a while, right?"

60

"During her junior year if I remember right. It wasn't for long because I dropped out."

"Did she tutor you up here?"

"Rochelle, you know there was never any physical relationship between me and Emmy."

"I know, but you did like her."

Rory walked out of the room as memories flooded his mind.

"Wait for me," Rochelle said and followed Rory down the stairs. He stopped near the bottom and sat down. She sat beside him.

"Did I strike a nerve?"

"You have to understand. For a couple years I had a thing for Diane, but she wasn't interested. I liked Emmy a lot, but not in that way. I'm pretty sure I never kissed her. We would hang out together. Especially if Kenny was on the road, but we never went on a date. Not ever."

"It's okay. I'm not jealous of her, or your relationship then or now. I can't say I ever had a deep friendship with another man that was purely platonic. My friends were females."

"I don't think I ever had a female friend other than Emmy."

Rochelle grinned and added, "From what I know about your past, I would say your interest in females was definitely not platonic."

"I'd erase that history in a second if I could."

Rory carried the last section of old carpet to the back of the yard. He dumped it on top of the pile and turned around.

"We knocked, but no one answered," Emmy said. "I heard the back door slam and thought you might be back here."

"Rochelle ran to the store to get more cleaning supplies, and I've been ripping out this old carpeting."

Emmy glanced at the pile long enough to see the color. "What? You're not keeping it. It looks so modern."

"You can have it if you want, Em. No charge."

"Thanks for the offer, Rory, but Emmy will pass," Kenny said. He turned and stared at the house. "How's the roof?"

61

Rory led them back toward the house and pointed. "That's about the only thing the previous owners replaced. The home inspector said it should last another ten to fifteen years. He said the electrical and plumbing were up to code, so I don't have to deal with that right now."

"Are you going to let us see the inside?" Emmy asked.

Rory opened the door and Emmy scooted past him. He took them on a tour, and they were returning to the first floor as Rochelle stepped inside the front door.

"What do you think, guys? Are we insane for taking on this project?" she asked.

Emmy answered, "I always thought with some effort..."

"And tons of money," Rory interrupted.

"Yes! Elbow grease, time and money and this place could be even better than when it was built. Kenny's parents' house is even older, and it's in great shape."

"I don't remember ever being inside this house," Kenny said as he ran a hand over the woodwork in the kitchen.

"You wouldn't have had any reason to," Emmy said. "I used to come over to see Amy."

"I've never been in the Colwell house unless it was for Halloween or something," Rory added.

"Maybe we could stop and show you the house after we eat. I haven't been by the house for several days," Kenny said. "Mom and Dad are in Florida, and I have to keep an eye on the place."

"The attic is one big room like the one here," Emmy said.

"Did you use it as your private domain?" Rochelle asked.

Kenny shook his head. "I used it to practice my guitar, but it was rather loud."

"Kenny and his father cleaned out the carriage house upstairs and that became the first rehearsal area for Fridays At Five," Emmy said.

"I heard it became the first for a few other things," Rory said to tease Emmy.

"Rory Porter, I should kick you in the shin," Emmy threatened.

62

"You shouldn't tease Emmy like that," Rochelle said wondering how many secrets her husband knew about Emmy.

"Yeah, Clarence, you shouldn't tease me."

Kenny grinned watching Emmy and Rory tease back and forth.

"Is anyone else ready for Darby's?" Rochelle asked.

"I have an idea," Kenny said holding up one finger.

"Praise be!" Emmy exclaimed putting her hands to her face. "That's the second one this year."

"We could eat at my parents' house. That would be easier than grabbing a booth at Darby's."

"If we know what we want, I could call in the order and Kenny could pick it up. We could walk to his house. It's chilly but not terribly windy."

Emmy placed the order, Kenny picked it up and brought it back to the Colwell house. He walked in as Emmy was finishing her tour.

"It was originally built in 1870 to replace a smaller house that burned."

"Dinner is here," Kenny hollered, "and how do you know all that, Em?"

"I did some research. Actually, Father James found it for me."

Kenny set the bags on the counter, and Emmy began pulling out their food.

"Did someone order a hot dog with ketchup?" Emmy asked holding it up.

"I did," Rory said grabbing it from her. "People down south like to use ketchup."

"Mr. Darby used to scowl at customers who wanted ketchup. He always told me it was only invented to put on fries."

"And you believed him?" Rochelle asked.

"I was only sixteen when I started working there. It was my first real job unless babysitting counts."

They sat at the small table to eat.

"Oh, Kenny, the bulb in the last bedroom on the right popped when I flipped the switch," Emmy said while pouring ketchup over her fries. "Could you change it please? I can't reach it."

"I can change it later. There aren't too many fixtures still using the old kind of bulbs."

"Have you switched to LEDs?" Rory asked.

Kenny chuckled and added, "I had to convince Dad it would save on his electric bill. He was skeptical at first, but it made a difference."

"I've always heard that older homes need more maintenance," Rochelle said.

"That's true, but our house is only fifteen years old..."

"We moved in at the end of May of 2005," Kenny corrected.

"Whatever!" Emmy gave him a look. "Fourteen, fifteen, doesn't matter. We've had to replace stuff already, and we've been thinking about finishing it."

Rochelle looked at Emmy and then Rory, who shrugged. "What do you mean, Emmy?"

"I'll answer since you have a mouthful of fries now, Em," Kenny said. "In the original plans there was a master bedroom suite on the ground floor."

"Really?" Rory asked.

Kenny described where the additional bedroom suite would have been.

"So, instead of a half bath at the end of the hallway, there would be doors leading into the master suite, right?" Rory asked.

"Exactly. It would be about the same size as what we have now, but without the need to climb stairs."

"Kevin complains his room isn't big enough," Emmy said. "He wants to use the guest room as his office space."

"What will you do with all the space upstairs after the kids grow up, get married, whatever and move out?" Rory asked.

"We could turn it into a bed and breakfast," Emmy said. "That would generate some income after Fridays At Five turns into a local bar band."

"I can't see that happening, Emmy," Rory said.

"They won't be a major rock act forever," Emmy said.

"I'm right here," Kenny said.

Rory shook his head. "No, I meant I can't see you operating a bed and breakfast. Cooking breakfast for strangers, making beds, cleaning bathrooms, stocking the pantry and whatever else people who run B&B's do."

"Why not? It wouldn't be much of a change. I already do all that."

"Except you don't cook for strangers, Em," Kenny said.

Saturday night as they were getting into bed, Emmy asked, "Do you have any plans for the guesthouse? It's been empty since Dany and Darian left."

"I don't know what to do with it. We used it as the band's office before, but we don't need that since Andy lets us use space in his building."

"In that case, I have an idea."

Kenny grinned at her.

"Not that!"

"What then?"

"Bobby keeps talking about finding a bigger apartment. His lease is up at the end of the month and he wants to move."

"It would be a big house for one person."

Emmy shook her head. "I don't think it would be just one person for long."

"Is he getting serious about Shay Brennan?"

"You can't tell anyone, but he bought a ring."

"That is serious," Kenny said with a sigh. "Has he popped the question yet?"

"Not yet, but there might be an issue if we rent the place to him."

"I think I see where you're going."

"We couldn't let Shay move in until they're married. Are we in agreement with that?"

"Definitely! It would set a bad example for the girls."

"And Kevin Michael, too," Emmy added. "Just because he's a boy doesn't mean... you know."

"Agreed. Have you mentioned the guesthouse to Bobby?"

"I told him it was empty. He laughed and said it would be a lot closer to the recording studio."

"Speaking of the studio, is there anything else you want to add?" Kenny asked.

"I want to listen to it one more time, but I think it's ready for a final mix and then it can be mastered. The artwork is ready as long as we don't change the track order."

"I don't want the guesthouse to stay empty much longer."

"I'll call him tomorrow before church," Emmy said turning off the light.

"What's so important that you needed to call so early?" Bobby asked. He looked at his clock. "It's only six thirty?"

"Did I wake you? Sorry," she said with a laugh. "I know you like to sleep late. You're always the last one out of his bunk on the bus. I have news and wanted you to hear it right away."

"Tell me."

"How would you like to move into the guesthouse?"

"How much?"

Emmy told him the amount.

"Are you sure?" he asked sitting up in bed.

"I know we could ask for more, but we let Dany stay there for the same price."

"I'll take it. When can I move in?"

"Before you start moving in, there is one rule."

"What?" he asked getting out of bed.

"Shay can't move in until you're married. You are planning to ask her soon, right?"

"Don't need to," Booby said.

"What? Why not? You didn't break up, did you?"

"Nope! I proposed last night, and she said yes."

"Congratulations, Bobby! I'm so happy for you."

"Thanks, Em. This time I'm ready to make it work."

"Good, but she still can't move in until you're married."

"I can live with that. I'll start packing this afternoon."

Chapter Seven

"Emmy, what brings you to Mercy?" Rory asked looking up from his computer monitor. "Is anyone sick or hurt?"

She waved a hand and sat in the chair in front of his desk. "Everyone is fine. James is working too much and doesn't get enough rest, but he's stubborn. I was upstairs visiting Adam and Juliana. She had a baby boy this morning. Do you remember Adam?"

"Of course. He was always the most serious guy on the bus."

"He's still like that."

"Doesn't he have a daughter?"

"Kinsey, and she's six. She wanted a baby sister, and asked her mother if she could trade with someone."

"Did she really?"

Emmy laughed. "No, but it makes for a good story, huh?"

"You should be a writer, Em."

She grinned and said, "I might think about it. How's the house coming? Did all your furniture arrive yet?"

"It did. We did our bedroom first, so we'd have a place to sleep."

"That comes in handy."

"You should see the hardwood floors. They turned out better than we thought possible. The new carpet was installed in the bedrooms, and everything downstairs has been painted. I did have to replace some of the plumbing in the upstairs bathroom."

"You?"

"Hey! I can do some things."

"If you say so."

"The rest of the bedrooms are empty, and the garage is beyond saving, but I got an estimate to have a new one built."

"Before the company was sold, I would call Tony and have him do all the remodeling and stuff. Now he works for Liberty Manufacturing and doesn't have the time."

"I never thought Bertucci and Keasling Construction would be sold to a company from out of state."

"It was a surprise, but I guess the offer was too good to turn down. I know Tony and Kristen got a big chunk of it. Derrick, too."

"Where does Derrick live now? I know he lived in Arizona for a few years then came back to SoHam."

"He and Amber are back in Phoenix. They spend time there and Florida and get back to SoHam once in a while to see Kristen and the kids."

"I always thought he was all right. He never acted like a rich kid in high school."

"Neither did Krissy, but she always wore nice clothes."

"Are you guys serious about adding on to the house?"

"Not this year, but we might after the kids are in college. We could close off the entire upstairs and save on utilities."

Rory laughed.

"Hey! We aren't making as much money now that the band isn't touring all the time and selling thousands of CDs."

"You mean millions."

"Whatever."

"Em, I know it's hard for you to forget about how you were raised, but you won't go broke anytime soon."

"I know, but something could happen to the economy."

Rory stared at her.

"Sometimes I forget God has everything under control, and I don't need to worry. He will supply all our needs."

"You could always sell the big house and live in the other one," Rory suggested.

"Can't. Bobby moved in. He and Shay are engaged and she will move in after the wedding."

"You're making her wait, huh?"

"How would it look to the girls if she lives with him?"

"You never lived with Kenny before you got married, did you?"

"No, but he wanted me to move into the carriage house instead of my apartment. I could have because he was always on the road and had a room in the house, but I just couldn't. It would have been too close to my mother."

Rory's phone rang and he took the call. Emmy looked around the office. She stood up to read the plaques and saw his diplomas. She sat down when he hung up.

"See! It's official. I am now Dr. Porter."

"Like I'm ever gonna call you that," she teased. She got serious and asked, "Did you regret not having kids?"

"Whoa! Where did that come from, Em?"

"I know how much you love my kids."

"I do and that's enough for us. Rochelle wanted children when she was younger, but it never happened. Now she is happy to borrow children for a time then give them back."

"I always figured I'd get married and have kids, but then I had... female issues... and my doctor told me I would be unlikely to have children."

"Thank God doctors aren't always right, huh?"

She paused, glanced at the floor and then up at him.

"What are you thinking, Em?"

"Seeing your old house brought back some memories," she answered.

"Good ones?"

"Mostly."

He waited for her to elaborate. Ten seconds passed like several minutes.

"Were you surprised I made it through high school without getting pregnant?" she asked softly.

"Wow! Another one from out of left field. Why would I assume you would get pregnant?"

"Because it happened to plenty of other girls from families like mine. I didn't exactly choose the best friends..."

"I was your friend," he said. "Kenny was your friend."

"Okay, I had two good friends."

"Good?"

"Great," she answered with a grin.

"Barry Newton. Tony Bertucci."

"Fine!"

"I admit Amy wasn't the best influence."

"I was older than her."

69

Rory leaned back in his chair. "Yes, but only in physical years. Birth years. Amy was far older than you in other ways."

"I used to think about you... after you moved away. Not all the time but once in a while. Someone would mention your name, or I'd go past your house, or I'd see, one of your old friends. Stuff like that." She looked at the ceiling for a moment before looking at him again. "Do you think God protected me from you? Did He make you leave SoHam?"

"I've heard that God works in mysterious ways, but what you're saying is pretty far-fetched, Em. I don't think God had anything to do with me leaving."

"Kenny used to tell me God had a plan for my life." She waved a hand. "Way before I gave my life to Him. Kenny would say God protected me at times from making mistakes, but there are many times in the Bible and in life now when He allows people to go their own way. Make terrible mistakes and suffer the consequences."

"Even I know we have to take responsibility for our actions," he said when Emmy paused.

"I've never understood why God singled me out. You know what I mean?"

"You're saying God stopped you from doing certain things, right?"

"He allowed Diane to make the mistakes..."

"She made the mistakes so you could learn from them."

"I suppose in a way that's true. I remember when she told me about having sex, and I said I was never gonna do that until I was married."

"You were just a kid."

"I was fourteen, so I knew enough."

He grinned and asked, "Was it difficult to keep that... vow?"

"Oh, hush!" She frowned at him. "If you'd been around, you'd know it was. If you had stayed in SoHam, it would have been even more difficult."

"Is that why you think God made me leave?" To remove temptation?" he asked and then chuckled.

70

"It's not funny. I'm fortunate that most of the male friends I had thought of me as a best bud."

Rory raised his eyebrows.

"Guys put some girls in the friend zone just like girls do."

"I never did that," he said.

"Yes you did! You put me there even though you teased me about doing stuff."

"What stuff?"

Emmy sighed.

"Oh, that stuff. I did tease you."

"Owen didn't tease. I always thought he would... you know."

"No way! He was five years older than you," Rory said shaking his hand. "Even he wouldn't stoop that low."

"Craig is five years older than Diane."

"You aren't Diane."

"No, but Owen and Craig were a lot alike."

"Yeah, they were... uh... jerks."

Emmy giggled and said, "Are you afraid to swear in front of me now? You weren't when we were kids."

"That was different. I didn't know any better."

"I heard that language at home all the time," she admitted.

"Hey! You used some language, too."

"I know, and I would punish the kids if I ever heard them using the same words."

"I can't imagine the girls talking like you did."

"I remember one time when I said a bad word in front of Kenny's parents."

"Which one?" he asked with a grin.

"The really bad one."

He shook his head. "No, which parent?"

"Oh, it was both of them, and I shocked them. You know how sometimes little kids repeat what they hear their parents say, and they're young enough to still be cute?"

"Yeah, I've seen that happen. It usually embarrasses the parents."

"I was old enough that I wasn't at the cute stage."

71

"Did they say anything?"

"They told Kenny not to swear."

"Do you use any four letter words in your books?"

"All the time," she answered with a grin.

"No, I don't mean words like 'that' and 'just.'"

"You'd know if you read any of the books," she said.

"I've read parts, but they aren't exactly my taste."

"That's because you aren't a young girl or a grandmother." She checked the time. "I gotta run. Call me sometime and we can get together to see what you've done with the house."

"Will do." He walked around the desk and hugged her.

"Say hi to Rochelle."

"Guess who called me this morning," Diane said Sunday afternoon while sitting on a barstool at Emmy's kitchen island. She rubbed the granite countertop. "You'll never guess."

Emmy shrugged and poured another cup of coffee for her sister. "How many tries do I get?" Emmy asked as she sat next to Diane.

"Carson and Caden's grandparents!" Diane exclaimed.

Emmy kept a straight face as she asked, "What's so unusual about Mona or Mr. Robertson calling. They live next door. At least when they aren't traveling the world."

Diane poked Emmy's arm.

"Ow! That hurt."

"You can be such a brat at times. You know perfectly well who I mean. Craig's parents called."

"What did they want?"

Diane huffed and said, "They want the boys to spend spring vacation with them in Florida. Can you believe the nerve?"

"Diane, they are still their grandparents even though you and Craig are divorced."

"Technically, I guess."

"No, not technically," Emmy said. "They are true blood grandparents. Did you tell Carson and Caden?"

"I told them."

"What did they say? Do they want to go?"

Diane shook her head. "They haven't seen them in ages. Caden said he doesn't like Craig's mother because she always treated him like a baby. However, she still sends birthday cards and a Christmas present."

"They kinda have a right to see them, you know?"

"No they don't! Craig might have a legal right according to the divorce settlement, but he doesn't bother. His parents don't have a right."

"You used to get along with them," Emmy said. She picked up an apple from the basket on the island and took a bite.

"Tolerated would be more like it. I had to when Craig and I were together. They would always buy the boys toys instead of the clothes they needed."

"That's what grandparents do. They spoil the grandkids. Kenny's parents are no different."

"Are they still in Florida?"

"No, they came back yesterday. Kenny and the kids are over there now." Emmy used the garbage disposal to get rid of the apple core. "They had planned to stay until May, but changed their minds."

"Do you think I should force the boys to see them?"

Emmy leaned against the counter. "I wouldn't. Carson is seventeen. He's old enough to decide."

Kevin Michael dashed through the garage, flew up the stairs, raced out of the mudroom and into the kitchen. "Mom! Dad! Come quick! You gotta see this."

Emmy tossed the dish towel at the counter. Kenny spilled a glass of water.

"Hurry!" Kevin yelled and then disappeared the way he came.

"What's going on?" Heather asked. She and Isabella followed Kevin.

"I'll wipe that up later," Kenny offered.

He and Emmy headed outside.

"Look!" Kevin shouted. "Grandpa bought a new car. Isn't it cool? It's bigger than his old one." He vanished into the interior of the dark blue SUV. "It's got three rows."

Kenny sighed.

Emmy shook her head. "We thought something was wrong."

"When did you do this?" Kenny asked approaching the new vehicle.

Kevin stuck his head out of the door and yelled, "There's seats in the back. There's enough room for all of us."

"Grandpa, why did you buy a new car?" Isabella asked.

"I wanted one we could all ride in together. This is a Honda Pilot and it has three rows of seats."

Kenny opened the driver's door and hopped in. "What trim is this?"

"It's a Pilot Elite."

"Why didn't you buy another minivan?" Emmy asked. "They have plenty of room."

Grandpa chuckled and answered, "I would have but Elly said she didn't want to drive a minivan anymore."

"Isn't this just as big?" Kenny asked.

"It's a little shorter, and it has AWD."

"You never go anywhere if there's snow or ice," Emmy said. "You head to Florida if you see a little flurry."

"Now I don't have to. We can stay later and see my precious grandchildren," he said giving Heather and Isabella a squeeze.

Chapter Eight

"Welcome back to Roosevelt High, Mrs. Colwell," Principal Davis Gorman said. "It's a pleasure to meet you."

Vice-Principal Mace Franklin grinned and said, "Davis, if you want to get on her good side, you will call her Emmy and not Mrs. Colwell."

"Please accept my apology," he said.

"It's all right. I'll give you the benefit of the doubt and pretend you were being polite," she said with a grin while shaking hands with Mace. "Good to see you again, Mace."

"We have time before the last class ends. Would you like a tour of the building? There have been some changes over the years."

"I noticed," Emmy said turning to face the entrance. "We didn't have metal detectors or a security guard when Mace and I were students."

"A necessary addition," Principal Gorman said.

"If you will excuse me, I need to talk to a student," Mace said. "Stop by the office before you leave."

"Why? Are you going to give me a detention?" Emmy teased.

He smiled and said, "If need be, but you need to return the visitor pass."

She touched the laminated 'V' and nodded.

"The first floor contains..."

Principal Gorman gave Emmy a fifteen minute tour of the three-story building which occupied an entire city block.

"How long have you been the principal?" Emmy asked when they returned to his office.

"This is my third year. Before that I was the superintendent of a much smaller school district in Iowa."

"You aren't from SoHam, right?"

The bell sounded, and he gently moved Emmy closer to the wall. "There will be a stampede in a few seconds."

"I remember how crowded the halls would be between classes. I got run over too many times to remember."

75

She watched as hundreds of students magically filled the hall. *Wow! High school kids certainly look a lot younger than when I went here.*

"My grandparents were originally from SoHam. I would visit in the summer, but I lived in Iowa. They were charter members of Crest Ridge United Nazarene. Mace mentioned that is your church."

"Really? What are their names? Would I know them?"

"You might have heard the names, but they moved to Alabama about thirty years ago. Only during the winter at first, but they've lived there full-time for fifteen years at least. Their names are Bob and Roseanne Gorman."

Emmy thought for a time. "Sorry, but I don't know the names. I've been going there regularly since 2001."

"It's a large church. I can see why it would not be possible to know everyone."

"Where does the writers group meet?" she asked after the crowd thinned out.

"I will escort you there. It's on the second floor. The faculty sponsor is Mrs. Matlock."

Emmy stopped and looked up at Principal Gorman. "Did you say Mrs. Matlock?"

"Yes. Why?"

"Is she a really short lady about the same height as me?" Emmy asked placing a hand on top of her head.

"You are about the same size. In height, I mean."

"She was my teacher in my senior year. Half the year. I graduated in January. I didn't know she still taught here."

"You make her sound ancient," he said and then laughed. "She had to have been rather young when she taught you."

"You are probably right. It's weird how students always assume their teachers are much older than they really are."

"This is the room," he said a moment later opening the door. "Mrs. Matlock, this is Emmy Colwell." Principal Gorman introduced Emmy.

"It's a pleasure to meet you," Mrs. Matlock said with a smile and a slight Scottish accent. "Please call me Sharon."

Emmy shook hands with the teacher, who couldn't be taller than five feet even in her comfortable shoes. "It's nice to see you again you, Mrs. Matlock. You were my teacher my last semester here at Roosevelt."

"You must call me Sharon, and I thought you looked familiar, but I didn't recognize the name Emmy Colasanti-Colwell."

"I was Emmy Colasanti until I got married. Emily Colasanti if you use my given name. I use Colasanti for my CDs, but I add the Colwell for the books."

Mrs. Matlock lightly tapped the front of her jaw and then grinned. "I remember you now. You were a very talented and conscientious student. The shyest in your class perhaps, but quite intelligent."

"I was definitely shy in class," Emmy admitted. "I have to admit I'm a bit nervous. I seldom talk to a room of people unless I'm singing with my band."

"You have no reason to be nervous, my dear. Few of the students bite, and they have expressed some jitters about meeting you."

"Do I look intimidating?" Emmy asked with a smile.

Mrs. Matlock laughed and whispered, "You look ferocious, my dear."

A few minutes later Mrs. Matlock told the students, who were milling about the room stealing surreptitious glances at Emmy, who was sitting on a stool, to take a seat. Most of them stared at Emmy as they sat at their desk.

"In case some of you have been hiding in a cave for the last few years, I would like to introduce today's guest speaker. I wrote this down to make sure I got the numbers right." She moved her reading glasses into place. "Okay, she has released nine CDs... Wow! That's a lot." Mrs. Matlock looked at Emmy. "But more germane to this organization she is the author of six books. Her latest book *That Is Not Possible, Is It?*, is the second installment in her series about high school students, Claire and Ruby." Mrs. Matlock looked up from her notes. "I'm proud and thrilled to introduce SoHam's very own Emmy Colasanti-Colwell."

77

Emmy giggled because some of the students stood up as they clapped. She moved to the wooden podium, set her index cards down and looked at the students.

"Thank you for that warm welcome. I'm a bit nervous, so please bear with me..."

"Go for it, Emmy!" one of the young men shouted.

Emmy mentioned the pertinent facts about her education and growing up in SoHam.

"I might have even had a class in this very room. Anyway, I don't want to bore you with details about my life. I'd rather answer any questions you might have."

A rather plump blonde in the first row waved a hand with enough enthusiasm to generate a breeze with the strength to rustle the papers on her desk. "Hi! My name is Farrah..."

"Hello, Farrah," all the students responded in unison.

Farrah ignored them and continued, "According to your website, your daughters are now teenagers, correct?"

Emmy nodded.

"Do they read your Claire and Ruby books?"

"They insist on reading everything I write. They are horrified at the thought of me using them as characters in any shape or form." Emmy waited for the laughter to subside. "My son could care less about my books."

Emmy pointed to another student with long, stringy red hair and a pair of glasses that instantly identified him as a ninth-degree nerd.

"Hello, my name is Hudson, and I write columns for the *Rough Rider Bulletin*. That's the school newsletter by the way." He shifted his weight from one foot to the other and talked slowly as if it pained him to release each word. "I was wondering if you base your characters on real people you knew, or met, or combinations of people, or are they total works of fiction?"

Emmy nodded as he asked his question and answered, "Yes." She instantly felt guilty because the room erupted in laughter she assumed was directed at Hudson. "Actually, that is a very thought-provoking question, Hudson. Thank you. I will try to explain..."

Emmy relaxed and answered questions for the next hour. Far beyond the thirty minutes she intended to stay.

Emmy returned to the tall stool in the corner, and Mrs. Matlock came to the podium.

"We should thank Emmy for staying well beyond the time we originally asked." She turned to Emmy. "Thank you so much, dear. I am proud to have been your teacher."

"How did it go?" Kenny asked later. "I see you survived in one piece."

"That was scarier than doing a concert in front of one of your crowds."

"You mean like twenty thousand adoring, screaming fans?" he asked with a grin.

Emmy rolled her eyes and said, "No, I meant in front of two hundred drunks at a local bar."

"Aw, Em, we play to larger crowds than that."

"Pastor Tyler, could I talk to you for a minute, please?" Emmy asked before worship band rehearsal the next evening. "Won't take long."

Andy Walker glanced at his Rolex. "Make it quick, cuz. Pastor and I were discussing his message from last Sunday."

"Sorry to interrupt, but this concerns church membership."

Tyler chuckled and said, "I'm not sure we can admit you as a member, Emmy," he teased.

"I'm already a member and so is he." She nudged Andy's side. "This is about charter members."

"There aren't many of those left. Most have already passed on to their eternal reward," Pastor Tyler said using his official voice.

"Does the church have a list of members from the beginning?"

Andy put his hands on Emmy's shoulders. "I can tell you've got something on your mind and will not be pleased until you have an answer. I will meet you in the music suite."

"There is a dusty book in one of the office filing cabinets listing all members by the year they joined the church."

79

Emmy looked up at Tyler and asked with wide eyes, "Don't you have it on the computer?"

"Yes, but I thought you might want to see the original hard copy."

"I only want to search for a couple names. Would that be too much trouble? We have a few minutes before practice starts."

"It won't take more than a few seconds. Let's take a shortcut to my office," he said turning around.

"I didn't know there was a shortcut. Is it like a secret passage?"

He chuckled.

"You're teasing me," she replied.

They entered the church office, and he sat at the church secretary's desk.

"Does Mrs. Crawford mind you using her computer?" Emmy teased.

"Are you going to tell her?"

"It will be our secret. What are the names?"

"Bob and Roseanne Gorman. According to their grandson they were charter members," she answered.

Tyler tapped a few keys. "Yes, here they are."

"Are they still alive?"

Tyler chuckled and answered, "Unless they've been called home in the last few hours, they are still among the living. I received an email from them yesterday."

"Have they been to church lately?" Emmy asked leaning over Tyler's shoulder to look at the list of charter members.

"Unfortunately, our attendance records do not include churches in Alabama."

"That's okay."

"Why the interest?"

"The principal at Roosevelt High is their grandson. I met him yesterday and he mentioned them."

"How did your meeting go?"

"Better than I imagined. The students asked lots of questions about writing, so I didn't have to talk about me all the time. The faculty sponsor taught me."

"How old is she?" Tyler asked.

"She's not that old! It wasn't like a thousand years ago that I was in high school."

"I get it. You are only four years older than me. Anything else you need to check?"

She backed up and said, "No, just those names."

Tyler closed the file and stood up. "Did you meet any students with potential as a writer?"

"There was this nerdy one. Hudson Ottewell."

"Nerdy?"

"Sorry, I shouldn't judge him, but he did look like one. Anyway, he asked several questions and I read one of his essays. He's got game."

"Good to know."

"Do you still have your wedding dress, Mommy?" Isabella asked in a whisper as Shay Brennan walked down the aisle Saturday morning.

"It's in a box in my closet. I thought maybe you or Heather might wear it one day," Emmy answered. She turned her attention from Shay Brennan and her father to the platform where Bobby O'Connor waited with his groomsmen. *I remember when we first met. You were such a punk. You're still a punk, but Shay will fix that soon enough.*

"Doesn't Shay look gorgeous?" Isabella asked. "And she smiled at me."

"She is a radiant bride," Emmy whispered.

"I love the way her hair is braided and her makeup," Heather said. "Did you wear makeup when you got married, Mom?"

"I had to. Diane wouldn't let me get away without it, and I spent a fortune getting my hair done. I wanted to wear it in a ponytail."

"Did you really?" Isabella asked.

"Not really, but it would have been easier."

An hour later Emmy cornered Bobby in the church's all-purpose room. "That was a nice ceremony. Short, but sweet."

"Did you time it, Em?"

"No, I made Kenny do it. Did you tell Shay you wanted a short ceremony?" she asked with a slight frown.

Bobby shook his head. "Shay had total control over it. I did what I was told. It was her first wedding."

"It was the first time you got married in the church," Emmy reminded him.

"Yes, and this time it's for the right reasons."

Emmy made a face.

"I married Maria just for the sex. It was a mistake."

"Maybe it's none of my business..."

"What do you want to know, Em? We've been friends for too long for 'me' to have any secrets."

"When is she due?"

"Geez, Em!" Bobby exclaimed looking around to see if anyone might have overheard Emmy's question.

"You haven't been engaged for a full month yet. I'm not stupid. Too many people in my family have been pregnant when they got married."

"She's due in early November."

Emmy poked him hard in the chest. "For Christ's sake, Bobby! Couldn't you wait?"

"Sorry, Em, but it wasn't all my fault. You should understand that."

"What do you mean by that, you punk?" she asked sternly. "Kenny and I waited if that's what you're insinuating. It wasn't easy, but we did."

He looked into her eyes. "Sorry, it's none of my business, but things are different now."

"That's crap! What kind of example are you setting for the young people in the church? Most of them can count to nine," she whispered as loudly as she could. She looked around to make sure no one was watching and smacked his arm. "I am disappointed in you." She stared into his eyes, took several deep breaths, sighed, hugged him and said, "I still love you even if you're a punk."

"Does that mean you won't fire me? Our baby will need a father with a job."

"You're lucky you're the only drummer who knows how to follow me."

"Are you going to tell Kenny or the girls?"

"Not now. If the girls do the math and ask questions, I won't cover for you."

"The baby might be premature," he said despite realizing Emmy would jump all over him.

"God knows all our sins, Bobby. You know that." She poked him again.

"Is it all right if Shay moves in today?" he asked with a grin. "We are married now." He held up his hand to show her the ring.

"She can move in, but tomorrow's Easter Sunday, and I expect to see you at church. No excuses."

"We will be there, Emmy. We can start our honeymoon Monday."

"You already started it, you punk." She turned and walked away. She saw Heather and Isabella talking to Shay. *I have to learn to be more forgiving. We are all sinners under grace.*

Chapter Nine

"Hi, Mom. We're home. School sucked today. Do we have anything good to eat. I looked in the pantry this morning and we're out of cookies." Kevin tossed his backpack and jacket on the kitchen island.

Emmy closed the fridge, saw the backpack and pointed to the mudroom. "We have fruit in the fridge and on the island. The pears are ripe."

He grabbed a pear, inspected it and stuck in in his mouth. He picked up his stuff and walked back to the mudroom. He returned and tossed the pear in the trash.

"Did you eat it already?" Emmy asked.

"Most of it. I was hungry." He walked past the kitchen desk and doubled back. He picked up a CD and showed it to his mother. "Was today the release day for this? Did you have a press conference this morning?"

"No, I didn't want to make a big deal about it."

"But Mom! You said it's your last CD. Shouldn't that be a big deal?" He checked out the cover, turned it over, looked at the list of songs and inspected the front again. "Where did you come up with the title? *Inadequate Ordinary People* is kinda weird."

"It's based on a sermon Pastor Tyler preached."

"I get it. It's like Moses. He claimed he wasn't smart enough to do what he did, right?"

"That and there are other examples of God using ordinary people to do extraordinary things with God's help."

"Are you gonna preach to me now? I had a bad day at school." He sat on a barstool and picked up another Bosc pear.

"Do you want to talk about it?" Emmy stood across the island from him. "I may not be your father, but I can listen."

"Promise you won't tell Heather or Isa?"

"I promise," Emmy said. She walked around the island and sat next to him. "Tell me what happened."

"Two of my so-called friends started teasing me," he said and stopped.

"What about?"

"They saw me talking to Gracie at lunch and told me she was my girlfriend. They told some of the other kids that I liked her and wanted to kiss her. Yuck! Gracie's a girl and she's my cousin."

Emmy grinned and whispered, "Gracie is a girl. A rather pretty one. She looks a lot like your aunt Kristen."

"Mom! You're not helping."

"You do know Grace is not really a blood cousin, right?"

"Yeah, I get that, but we've grown up like cousins. She's okay for a girl, but I'd never want to kiss her."

"Is there a different girl in your class you'd rather kiss?"

"Mom!" he exclaimed getting up. "If you're gonna be like that, I'm going to my room. Even if I liked another girl, I wouldn't tell you about it. You'd tell Heather, and she'd torture me and make my life miserable."

"I'm sorry. I know life can be difficult at your age."

"How can you know? You're an adult."

She put an arm around his waist, pulled him close and said, "Believe it or not, I was once the same age as you, and I felt confused at times. Most of the time if I'm honest."

"I know you were a kid, Mom, but like in ancient times."

Emmy looked at him and saw a grin. "I know you're teasing me. It was your father that was a kid in ancient times. I'm much younger than him."

"Younger than who?" Isabella asked as she walked by.

"I was telling your brother how much younger I am than your father," Emmy explained.

"I thought you were only three and a half years younger than Daddy," Isabella said. "He and Heather are still outside. Bobby and Shay were going for a walk, and they stopped to talk."

Heather entered the room and tossed her backpack on the desk. "Is it true Shay's going to have a baby?"

"Where did you hear that?" Emmy asked.

"Bobby told Daddy last week," Heather answered. "They aren't waiting forever like Dany and Darian did."

"Some people are ready to have a baby as soon as they get married. Others like to wait until they've been married for a few years."

"Are you trying to tell me something, Mom? I know girls can get pregnant before they get married. It's called having sex." Heather grinned because she knew it would embarrass her mother.

"Is Shay expecting?" Isabella asked. "That was fast."

"It only takes one time to get pregnant," Heather said.

"Geez! I'm leaving if you're gonna talk about that stuff," Kevin said. He shuddered and quickly ran upstairs.

"Heather Rose, that's no way to talk."

"But it's true, isn't it, Mom?"

"Yes, and some girls make mistakes."

"I once heard Grandma telling Aunt Diane you were a mistake. Were you?"

Emmy bit her lip as she remembered something her mother said many years ago. She regained her composure and said, "I was unexpected because of your grandmother's age, but I was not a mistake. God does not make mistakes."

"What about babies who are born deformed and stuff like that?" Heather asked.

"Those babies are special, and God loves them just as they are."

"Even more?" Isabella asked.

Emmy shook her head. "I'm pretty sure God loves all of us exactly the same."

"Even Kevin Michael?" Heather asked putting her hands to her face as if in shock. "He's so weird. I saw him carrying Gracie's books last week."

"For real?" Emmy asked.

"Yeah, and they were talking to each other."

"He was probably just trying to be helpful," Isabella said.

"Someone still believes in fairy tales," Heather said walking away.

Kenny stuck his head into the den the next afternoon and asked, "Are you busy?"

She held up a finger and continued typing for several seconds. "I'm working on the outline for the next book. What's up?"

86

"Kevin told me about some kids teasing him about Grace. Did you know about this?"

"He told me yesterday. What did you tell him? Something useful and full of fatherly advice I hope."

"I told him you and I were friends when we were kids."

"How did he react to that?"

"Are you asking so you can use it in a book, or as his mother?"

Emmy bit her lip and said, "Both, if I have to be honest. It's hard to write as a contemporary teenager. Things have changed so much since you and I were that age."

"Yeah, kids have cell phones, computers and instant socializing now. We had to communicate via face-to-face talking."

They talked about Kevin until Emmy's cell phone rang. She checked the caller ID and said, "It's Annie O'Dell. I should talk to her."

"I'll do some research, so I can talk to Kevin and the girls using current teen lingo."

Emmy shook her head. *You're such a dork.* "Hi, Annie, how are you?"

"Did I call at a bad time?" Annie asked. "Are you too busy to talk?"

"This is a perfect time. I was working on an outline and need to take a break. How are you and Matt. Keyshon must be growing up so fast if he's like my kids."

"Everyone is fine. Keyshon will be eight in August and Alanna just turned two. She drives me crazy at times. She has learned to say no to everything."

Emmy closed her eyes. *Shoot! I forgot you had a daughter. I'm a terrible friend.*

"I'd like to talk to you about something serious if I may."

Emmy opened her eyes and sat up. "Of course. What is it?"

"Could we get together and talk in person. I'd rather not discuss it over the phone."

"I'm free whenever you are," Emmy said. "That's an advantage of being a writer. I can change my schedule whenever I need."

"I shouldn't be so mysterious. The truth is I'm expecting and not sure if I can go through with having the baby."

"Why?" Emmy exclaimed. "Are you sick or something?"

"I'm fine, but we got the results from a test, and it's probable that the baby has Down Syndrome. I'm not sure I can deal with that after losing Mace's brother."

"I can meet you now if you'd like," Emmy said closing her laptop and standing up.

"I can't today because I have parent-teacher conferences after school. Would you be free after school tomorrow?" Annie asked.

"I have worship band rehearsal, but that's not until seven. I'm free after school."

They agreed to meet at the Barclay Academy where Annie taught students with developmental challenges.

Good! This will give me a chance to check out the school again. I really think it would benefit Heather and Isabella to attend high school there. Emmy closed her eyes and prayed for Annie, Matt and the baby.

"Thank you for meeting me here," Annie said the next day. "We could use my office or there is a Beanz 'n' More down the street if you'd prefer."

"Your office is fine," Emmy said. "How do you like working for Bennett Robertson? He's Diane's brother-in-law."

"I like him. He's brought the Academy into the modern age."

Annie led Emmy into her small office, closed the door and took a seat behind her desk. Emmy sat on one of the stackable office chairs in front of Annie's desk and looked at the photos on the wall behind Annie.

"The kids are growing and Alanna looks a lot like you," Emmy said.

"She does according to my father. He claims she is exactly like me at that age."

"How is your father? He retired from the police force a while back, didn't he?"

"He and Elisabeth are both retired. You know they built a house on Grandpa's farm, right?"

"I remember that. I've been to your grandfather's farm. He took care of Daddy once when Mom kicked him out," Emmy said. "But that's not important. I want to talk about the baby."

Annie wiped away a tear. "Do you think I'm horrible for even thinking about not having the baby because he might not be perfect?"

"Not at all, Annie. I don't know how I would react in your situation."

Annie watched to gauge Emmy's expression and shook her head. "Emmy, I know exactly how you would react. You would love the baby even more because of the issues. Don't tell me I'm wrong."

"It's because of my faith in Christ that I feel that way," Emmy said. "You know I was never supposed to be a mother, yet I've been blessed with three miracles." Emmy chuckled and added, "They aren't perfect and the girls are teens now. They've started their periods and are going through all the stuff we did at that age. Is that too much info?"

"Not at all. I will have to deal with that at some point with Alanna if she survives her terrible twos."

"Kenny's mom always tells me it will get easier, but she just says that to make me feel better." Emmy grinned hoping to make Annie feel more at ease.

Annie waited until a school wide announcement finished and said, "I don't know if I have the strength to deal with a baby after spending my days with my special needs students."

"How does Matt feel?"

"He says it's my decision and will support me no matter what. Secretly, I think he wants the baby."

Emmy closed her eyes for just a second, then said, "There's a song on my new CD that talks about God using inadequate ordinary people to do extraordinary things."

"You mean Moses?"

"Moses was one. David and Paul were two others. I mention Gideon and Jeremiah, too."

"I'm not real familiar with people from the Bible other than Jesus and Mary," Annie admitted.

Emmy told her how God used ordinary people to accomplish His will.

"But those were special cases. I'm not like that."

"They became special people because they allowed God to work through them."

"Does God work extraordinary things through you, Emmy?"

Emmy thought about Annie's question before answering, "He can accomplish things far beyond what we are capable of. I can't do anything without God. God does the work. I just allow Him to guide me in small ways."

"You are pretty humble considering all the amazing things you have accomplished."

Emmy felt her face turn red.

"I don't mean you sound insincere. Quite the opposite. You may not realize how much people look up to you. Most of the time free advice is worth just that, but I value your opinion because I know your life has been changed by your relationship with God."

"You can have that same relationship, Annie. I don't mean to preach at you, but I do care for you."

"You mean my eternal soul, huh?"

"Yes, I suppose, but I care for you as a person. I admit I get so busy with my life that I don't always remember to pray for my friends as much as I should."

"Everyone is busy, Emmy. You are the only person I know who thinks more about other people than yourself. Do you know what I mean?"

"God commands us to love Him with all our heart, soul and mind, and to love our neighbors as ourselves."

"I know that means more than just the people next door. I get along with my neighbors, but I can't say I ever think about the people who live on the next block or even down the street."

"It's an attitude we learn when we become more like Jesus," Emmy said. "Are the doctors absolutely sure about the baby?"

"The test is pretty accurate. How would I survive if the baby dies early like Keyshon Franklin did?"

"He lived a full life in the few years he had," Emmy whispered. "Do you think Keyshon would feel his life wasn't worth living?"

Annie's eyes filled with tears. Emmy jumped up, raced around the desk, grabbed a tissue from the box next to photos of Annie's children and dried Annie's tears. "I didn't mean to make you cry," Emmy said through her own tears.

"I'm being selfish, aren't I?" Annie asked. "Other than you, Keyshon was the best person I've ever known. He never thought of himself as disabled or handicapped. He would hate me if I chose to be weak and not have my baby."

"I think he would," Emmy said.

Annie stood up and hugged Emmy.

"Do you feel better now?" Emmy asked after the hug ended.

"Yes, and thank you for everything you said. I hope God will forgive me for even thinking about not having the baby."

"He loves us and will forgive us no matter how stupid we are at times. I've make tons of mistakes in my life, and He forgives me all the time. I think sometimes I must make Him laugh because I do such goofy things."

"You are quite extraordinary, Emmy. Thank you for being my friend."

"Stop it! You're gonna make me cry," Emmy said.

Annie hugged her again.

Chapter Ten

Emmy drove to South Hampshire's Gordon Hill neighborhood and parked alongside the warehouse Fridays At Five used for rehearsals and storage. The band bought the building from Jeff Rawlings' father in 1995 and used it to store their gear between tours. Emmy parked the car and hurried over to the side door. She punched in the code, 0-7-0-8-8-0, her birthday, and waited for the light to turn green. When it didn't she sighed. *Shoot! They changed the code.* She punched in the new code, 0-8-8-0-7-0, which was her birthday in reverse and opened the steel door. *It would take a burglar less than a second to break this code.* She could see the stage, which stretched over eighty feet wide and forty feet deep, complete with sound, lighting and pyrotechnics set up at one end of the 55,000 square foot building. Stage lights flashed as one of the tech guys ran through cues. She saw Kenny talking to Nelson Grapella and hurried over to join them. Nelson saw her first because Kenny had his back to her.

Nelson tapped Kenny's arm. "Your wife is here."

Kenny turned and smiled as Emmy approached.

"What are you doing here? I thought we were using the warehouse in the mornings?" Emmy asked.

"Nice to see you, too. I thought I would surprise you."

She kissed him and waved at her tour manager. "Am I the last one here?" she asked Nelson.

"We are still waiting for Bobby. He texted to say he will be here soon. He's running behind because of Shay not feeling well."

Emmy looked at Kenny. He shrugged to indicate he knew nothing.

"We can wait," Emmy said. "We have all week to rehearse and my material isn't that complicated to play."

Bobby O'Connor arrived ten minutes later and Emmy saw him first.

"Sorry, Em. I was ready to leave when Shay got sick."

"Is she okay?"

"She's all right. Just the normal... you know... morning stuff."

"I was going to blame your tardiness on you wanting to stay in bed too long if you know what I mean."

"Wasn't that, Em," Bobby said with a smile.

The warehouse stage easily held the gear for both bands. Thirty minutes after arriving, Emmy's front of house mixer, Bruce Sutherland, announced that everything was ready.

Emmy climbed the stairs to the stage and smiled at everyone. "Isaac, did everyone give you a hard time because you're the newest member of the band?"

"Em! Would we do that?" Bobby sat twirling a drumstick on the drum riser in the middle of the stage.

"Yes, you would. That's why I'm asking." She turned to Isaac, who was positioned to her right and slightly behind the first line of musicians. "Did that punk give you a hard time?"

Isaac Ladlow had originally been a member of the teen worship band at Crest Ridge United Nazarene. He agreed to join Emmy's band after graduating from Olivet Nazarene University with a dual degree in Music Composition and Performance.

Isaac smiled shyly and said, "They didn't tease me too much."

Boyd Goldman, one of three guitarists, laughed and said, "How can we tease him? He knows more about music than the rest of us put together. He can play all our instruments, the violin and he can sing any part. He knows all the music theory stuff that's like Greek to us."

Isaac looked at his bank of keyboards without responding.

Mason Williams, the bass player, said, "Isaac showed me how to do this." Mason played a complicated bass run. "Pretty amazing, huh?"

"We used to think Tommy was shy, but Isaac takes shyness to a whole new level," Paul Mahnari, another guitarist, said.

Tommy Joseph, twenty-one year old son of Fridays At Five guitar player, P.J. Joseph, laughed and shredded his guitar. "I let my playing talk for me."

Boyd tried to repeat the riff on his guitar, but failed.

Paul tried with less success.

Emmy looked at Isaac.

93

Isaac didn't say anything as he repeated the riff on one of his keyboards.

"That sounded just like a guitar," Bobby shouted. "How did you do that?"

"It's a sample," Isaac answered.

"But you still have to play it, right?" Boyd asked.

Isaac nodded.

Emmy looked at Boyd and smiled thinking of the man who had been part of 'The Only Hope' from the beginning only to lose his way and succumb to an addiction. *I'm so glad to have you back on the team. In a way, what you went through has strengthened you and now you have quite a testimony for young people facing the same demons.*

"Em, are you ready?" Rutger Sebastian asked through her in-ear monitors.

Emmy waved at Rutger, turned to look at Bobby and shouted, "Count it off."

He did, and Emmy's band roared through five numbers without even pausing between songs. Emmy used the extended solos to sip on tea sweetened with honey.

They took a break and Boyd asked Isaac, "How do you know all the material already? I got lost a bunch of times on the new songs."

"I have a good memory," Isaac answered.

"Are you going to play the violin on some of the songs?" Bobby asked.

"Emmy asked if I would," he answered.

Bobby nudged Boyd, grinned and asked, "Can you play the violin and the keyboards at the same time?"

Isaac chuckled softly and shook his head.

"See there, Emmy, he can't play two instruments at the same time," Bobby said.

"I wouldn't talk, punk," Emmy responded. "You can't talk and walk at the same time. When I first met you, you had trouble playing anything that wasn't four on the floor. You played the same pattern for every song."

"Not my fault worship music is all in 4/4 time."

Emmy told the musicians to take a break so she could go over vocal arrangements with Susan Lemmert and Tariq Jones. Isaac played a keyboard and helped with the arrangements.

"If you don't sing with us, I'm going to act like a real diva and throw a fit," Emmy told Isaac. "I could pay you an extra dollar or two."

Isaac grinned and said, "I could sing to fill in the lower parts since none of the other guys are singing."

Emmy looked over her shoulder at the other musicians who were joking around on the other side of the stage. "They can all sing. Even Bobby, but they're too lazy to learn the new material."

By noon Emmy and the band had rehearsed over half of the material for her summer tour. The guys from Fridays At Five arrived and joined everyone on the stage.

"You sounded pretty good for a local band," Jeff Rawlings said climbing the steps. "Now it's time for the pros to take over."

"Jeff! What are you doing here? You aren't supposed to be playing," Kenny said.

Everyone, including Emmy and her band, circled around Jeff.

"My doctor said I can't tour, but he never said I couldn't hang out with you." He shook hands with Ryan Lederer, who would be replacing him for the summer tour, and said, "Don't make me look too bad. I don't want them to think they can replace me so easily."

"No one could ever replace you, ol' buddy," Jeremy Lenhart said. "Believe me we've tried for over twenty years."

Near the end of rehearsal Friday morning Emmy took a sip of tea and smiled at her brother. "What do you think?"

Father James was hanging around so Emmy could take him to Darby's. He shrugged and said, "I'm not a musician, but I like your sound. Everyone starts together most of the time, and they end around the same time." He pointed to Bobby. "Except for him. He keeps playing a drum solo after everyone else finishes."

"That's because he's just learning how to play, Father James," Boyd teased.

95

Emmy listened to the banter between bandmates for a time and then bit her lip.

"What's up, Em? Why the weird smile?" Bobby asked. "Hey! Are you crying?"

Emmy used the back of her hand to wipe her eyes. "No, it's allergies, punk."

"Uh huh," Bobby said. "The ragweed is pretty thick in here."

"I stopped singing on that last song just to listen to you guys. You are amazing, by the way. This has to be the tightest band I've ever sang with, and I'm sad because it will be my last one."

"What do you mean?" Boyd asked sensing something serious was happening.

"The summer tour will be it for me. I'm retiring from the road. I'm getting too old, and I want to concentrate on my writing and stay home with the kids. They're growing up too fast."

"Em! You aren't even forty yet," Bobby said. "Look at Mariah Karney and some of those other singers. They have to be close to sixty."

"Fifty maybe," Paul replied. He used his phone to check the Internet. "Fifty at the most."

"Whatever! Emmy, you are too young to retire."

"Don't worry, Bobby," Boyd said. "I'm sure there's a bar band somewhere that would hire you to play on weekends once a month."

Emmy talked to the guys for several minutes about why she decided to retire.

"So, you're still going to sing at church, right?" Bobby asked.

"Yes, I will still be part of the worship team."

The guitar players packed their instruments, Isaac shut down his keyboards and Bobby turned off the mixer by his drums. Emmy and Father James stood by the stairs.

"You shouldn't make promises you might not be able to keep, little sister," Father James said.

"What do you mean? I'm not going to be like those artists who have reunion tours whenever they need the money. Once I retire, that's it. I'm finished traveling."

"Who knows how the future will turn out? I'm just saying you might change your mind at some point. Maybe you could play concerts without leaving SoHam."

"Yeah, and ten people might show up to hear me."

"Are you singing just for yourself?"

"Don't go all pious priest on me. You know why I sing. I could write lyrics like Kenny that hide his faith, but I don't."

"Maybe not at first, but I read the lyrics to your new material. It's pretty deep and not at all like those early worship songs."

"They aren't seven-eleven songs," Emmy said.

"I know what those are. Seven words sung eleven times."

"I'm not putting those songs down, but I... Oh, never mind. I'm hungry. Are you buying?"

Father James sighed and said, "I am but a poor man of the cloth."

Emmy shook her head. "I know you paid cash for your new car. Don't give me that poverty crap."

"I traded in my Civic. So the CR-V didn't cost that much," he replied.

"Kevin, are you ready to go?" Kenny hollered up the stairs. "I promised Mr. Robertson we would be there by nine."

"It's Saturday, Dad! Why did I have to get up so early?" Kevin asked dragging himself down the stairs.

"It's the Memorial Day weekend, and Mr. Robertson is leaving for Idaho this afternoon. Don't you want to see his new building. He has lots of antique cars."

"Can't we see them later? Is the building like Fort Knox?"

"Close. Grab some breakfast and we'll head over there."

Kevin opened the fridge, grabbed two donuts and a bottle of water. "I'm ready."

Bill and Mona Robertson lived across the road, though it would take several minutes to walk there. Most of the properties in the development were at least ten acres in size and covered in woods and hills. Mr. Robertson originally owned the 120 plus acres that became Bristol Ridge, and had retired after selling Robertson Industries in 2010 to a German company for over 800 million dollars. He and his second wife, Mona, lived in Bristol Ridge next to his son and grandchildren, when not traveling the globe.

Mr. Robertson waited next to his new building. His face shone with pride as Kenny and Kevin approached.

"Is it really full of old cars?" Kevin asked running toward Mr. Robertson. "Dad said you collect them. Do you?"

"I have several you might call old," Mr. Robertson answered.

Kevin watched the over-sized garage door roll up and peeked inside. "Wow! You do have a lot of cars. I thought we had too many, but you've got a hundred cars."

Mr. Robertson flipped on the lights. "Not quite that many."

Kenny looked at some of the posters on the walls. "It reminds me of Jay Leno's garage. He does those YouTube videos and shows off his collection."

"He's been collecting cars longer than me."

"What is that?" Kevin yelled as he raced toward one of the cars.

"That's a 1937 Cord," Mr. Robertson explained as he flipped on more overhead lights.

Kenny walked over to another car. He touched the chrome strip running from the headlight housing to the door handle. "Is this it?" he asked over his shoulder.

"That's it," Mr. Robertson answered. "A 1958 Packard Hawk. Not too many of those left."

"Is this a car from the future?" Kevin asked.

"Far from it," Kenny said with a laugh. "This car belongs to your mother."

"Really!? How come I've never seen her drive it? Did she just buy it?"

"No, it was given to her by a man who lived next door when she was younger."

Kevin walked around the Hawk. "It's got funny wings in back."

"Those were called fins back in the day," Mr. Robertson explained. He told Kevin all he knew about one of the last cars to bear the Packard name.

"How come I've never seen it before?" Kevin asked looking inside the car.

"It arrived two days ago," Mr. Robertson said. "It was in California being restored."

"How long has it taken?" Kenny asked. "I can't remember offhand."

"Almost ten years. Some of the parts were nearly impossible to find according to Jay."

"Can we take it for a ride?"

"Not today, Kevin. I think your mother should drive it first."

Kevin looked down at the floor. "I've never seen a garage floor that shined like this. It actually looks wet, and it's got sprinkles in it."

"It makes it easier to keep clean," Mr. Robertson explained.

"Do all these old cars still work?" Kevin asked.

"Yes, and I try to use them once a month at least."

"I think I've seen you drive this one," Kenny said.

"That's a 1958 Chrysler Imperial. It actually belonged to my father. He gave it to me when I turned eighteen. I've kept it ever since."

Kenny and Kevin checked out a 1948 Packard convertible.

"Do you have any old fire trucks?" Kevin asked.

"Sorry, Kevin, but so far I've only collected cars."

"They're not all old cars," Kenny said pointing to one in the corner.

"Oh, that," Mr. Robertson said with a laugh. "I figured I might need a more modern car some day."

Kevin stared at the red vehicle.

"It's a 2017 Ferrari 488 Spider. It's only got 1200 miles on it, but I plan to drive it occasionally. I'm not going to let it set idle. Cars are meant to be driven."

"Have you taken this to the SoHam Autobahn Club?" Kenny asked.

"Only once. It's more car than I can handle. I like driving ones like this." He led Kenny to another old car.

"Is that a real Duesenberg?"

"It's a 1930 J Walker La Grande Torpedo Phaeton. It's been fully restored, and I picked it up from a family in Indianapolis. They were the original owners."

"Doesn't it have a top, and why are there two windshields?" Kevin asked. "Can I sit in it?"

"Don't touch it, Kevin," Kenny ordered.

"He can get in," Mr. Robertson said.

"Okay, but don't touch anything on the inside."

Mr. Robertson opened the door, and Kevin carefully climbed inside.

"What do you think?" Mr. Robertson asked.

"Does it play MP3s?"

"I'm afraid not, Kevin," Mr. Robertson explained more."

"You mean this thing is older than you and Grandpa?" Kevin asked incredulously.

"Several years older," Kenny said. "Do you plan to buy more cars? You still have lots of room."

"I might buy a few more, but only if I find something that interests me. Some collectors I know buy Corvettes and Porsches and exotic Italian cars, but I prefer the old American-built ones."

"Can I go for a ride if you drive that one?" Kevin asked.

"Sure. We can take it out now if you have time."

Kevin looked at his father.

"Just drop him off at home, Mr. Robertson," Kenny said.

"Yeah! I get to ride in a doozie burger," Kevin hollered.

"Have you thought about what we talked about the other day?" Emmy asked after dinner Friday night.

Kenny closed his book. "What was that?"

She sat in her recliner. "Someone to watch the house this summer. I know there is security for Bristol Ridge, but I don't want the house to be empty all summer. The security guys can't be everywhere, and if I ask Shay to stay here, then the guesthouse is empty. Bobby will be with me, remember?"

"I agree with hiring someone, but who? Do you have anyone in mind?"

"Diane was getting after Carson because he doesn't have a job lined up for summer. He said he would look later, but he doesn't drive yet."

"Why doesn't he drive? He's seventeen, right?"

Emmy shrugged and answered, "Diane said he hasn't taken the class he needs. I got my license before I had a car."

"You drove mine when I was gone."

Emmy grinned and said, "I drove it more than you knew about. Once I got pulled over and had to flirt my way out of a speeding ticket."

Kenny shook his head. "I don't want to know, and how fast were you going? It was a Honda Civic. Not exactly known for speed."

"I don't remember, but whatever I did worked. I've never gotten a ticket."

"Who says God doesn't perform modern miracles."

"So what about hiring Carson to watch the house?"

"Watch it, or stay in it?"

"He could live here and just go home to eat."

"How much would we pay him, Em?"

"I could google it."

"What?"

Emmy rolled her eyes. "Google. It's a neologism."

"What in heaven's name does that mean? Are you making it up?"

"Google?"

"No, the other word. I know how to google something."

Emmy giggled and said, "I saw that other word when I was doing research for my book. I had to look it up because I had no clue. I think I'll use it in normal conversation just to see if anyone is honest enough to ask what it means. There are some people who wouldn't admit to not knowing something to save their life."

"Are you referring to me?"

"Not you. You are smart enough to realize you are clueless, dear."

101

"Real funny, Em. It's okay with me if you talk to Diane about Carson. You'll have to make a list of things to do. I don't want to pay him for watching TV and stuffing his face."

"We're leaving Tuesday. We have to decide tomorrow."

Emmy walked to Diane's house the next morning. She rang the doorbell and walked in. "Anyone home?" she hollered from the entryway.

Brady Robertson appeared from the kitchen carrying a cup of coffee and a piece of cheese coffeecake. "Hi, Emmy, is Diane expecting you?"

"Not really, but I want to talk to her about Carson."

Emmy explained what they wanted.

"Are you sure?"

"I think he would do a good job." Emmy heard someone coming down the stairs and laughed. "Are you just now getting out of bed?"

Diane made a face. "Shut up. Today was the first chance I've had to be lazy all week. Why are you here?"

Emmy explained everything again as they sat in the kitchen.

"He's too young," Diane said to close the conversation.

"No he isn't," Emmy insisted. "He's seventeen, and you want him to get a job, right?"

"Yes, he needs to learn responsibility."

"What better way to learn than this? He will be close, and you can check up on him."

"So, you want me to make sure he doesn't have girls over, huh?"

Emmy crossed her arms over her chest. "I hadn't thought of that, but I don't want him to have parties."

"What about the pool? Is he supposed to take care of that?"

"We have a service. I made a list of everything he would be responsible for." She handed the list to Diane.

Diane read it while drinking her coffee.

"Where are the kids, anyway?" Emmy asked.

"Next door with Grandma and Grandpa."

102

"Did you hear that Mr. Robertson gave Kevin a ride in his Duesenberg?"

"Is that what he was talking about. All I heard was something about a doozie hamburger."

"We kinda need an answer today," Emmy said.

"And if I say no?"

"I was gonna ask Andy to stay in the house."

Diane laughed.

"Okay, he wouldn't do it. He hates to leave his house."

"Have you even asked Carson?"

"I texted him this morning. I figured he would answer a text faster than calling him."

"What did he say?"

"He expressed an interest," Emmy said slowly.

"His exact words, or characters, Em," Diane ordered.

Emmy pulled out her phone and opened the text. "He said, 'Sure. Whatever.' That sounds like a yes to me."

Diane thought about it as she refilled her coffee. "If Brady will agree, I will allow it on a trial basis."

"Yes!" Emmy pumped a fist.

"What do I have to agree on?" Brady asked refilling his coffee.

Emmy explained faster than he could understand, so Diane interpreted.

"Oh, that," he said. "I think he would do a great job. Make the checks out to me."

"I was gonna give him cash," Emmy said.

"He will eat everything in the house," Diane said.

"That's a good thing. We will be gone all summer. See ya. He knows all the codes already."

Chapter Eleven

"The bus is here!" Kevin Michael hollered from the garage. "I get to choose my bunk first."

"You're the only one who has a bunk, Kevin," Heather said. "Mom and Daddy and Isa and I have bedrooms."

"Even better! I won't have to put up with you two."

The summer Fridays At Five tour would open the next day in Memphis, Tennessee. Emmy and her band would be the opening act for all dates.

"Did you remember to pack enough clean underwear?" Emmy asked the girls.

"Mom! We aren't babies," Heather said turning on her heels and walking away.

"Mom, we packed everything but our winter clothes," Isabella said. "I packed a jacket just in case."

"This is the first time we've all traveled together for a whole summer," Emmy said. "I wish we could have always toured this way."

Four hours later Heather walked into the front lounge of the bus, plopped down heavily onto the leather couch and sighed.

"What's wrong?" Emmy asked closing her laptop.

"This is the first day, and I'm already bored out of my mind."

"Kevin and Isa are playing a game. You need to find something to do besides sulk."

"Is this how it will be all summer. We are trapped in this crappy bus with nowhere to go and nothing to do? Why couldn't we fly like we used to?"

"It's too expensive to fly everywhere," Emmy said, "and this is a Prevost coach. It's one of the best there is."

"It's still a bus, Mom. It will take forever to get from place to place."

"After today we will be traveling at night. You will wake up in a different city most mornings."

"Will we have time to do stuff, or do you and Daddy have to work all day?"

"We will have a few hours of free time each day. You've been on tours before. You should know we have responsibilities just like any job or career."

"Sometimes I wish you and Daddy had normal jobs," Heather said with a sigh.

Emmy rubbed Heather's back. *If we had normal jobs, you wouldn't live where you do.* "Do you remember watching the video when Rory played the tambourine with us?"

Heather laughed. "He looked like a robot. He barely moved his arm, and then he tripped and did a somersault, got back to his feet and kept going like nothing happened. That was fun!"

"It's the little things like that you remember from the days on the road. Traveling from place to place. Living out of a suitcase. Eating the same old food every meal. None of that is easy, Heather. Not even in a plane."

"What are we supposed to do while you and Daddy are performing? Please say we won't be stuck at the hotel all night."

"You could help with one of the departments. You like clothes. You could help Sara White in the wardrobe department."

"Right! I would love to wash and iron clothes all day and night."

"Sara does more than that."

"Is Stephanie going to be there?"

Stephanie Grachan, a single mother, was the head of press relations for both bands. She raised four sons by herself. The oldest had turned fifteen in April and the youngest was six.

"She and Deveron will be on the tour. Stephanie will be working..."

"What about Dev? Does he have a job?"

"He helps his mother at times, but he's too young to be an employee."

"He's fifteen," Heather said.

"Yes, and that's too old for you."

"Mom! I don't think of him like that! He's a friend. Kinda like you and Barry Newton. You were always friends with him, but I doubt you ever kissed him," Heather teased.

"Deveron is not like Barry. He plays soccer, and Stephanie

105

says he really good. He can run faster than anyone on his team.

Heather fanned the air. "Boring."

"You better be nice to him. You might have to see him all summer."

"Speaking of Barry Newton, how old is Fender now?"

Emmy tilted her head. "Good question, Heather. I think he was born in early 2003."

"Oooh! He's sixteen, huh?"

"He is much too old for you, Heather Rose Colwell!" Emmy asserted emphatically.

"He is, huh? How much older is Daddy than you?"

"That's different and you know it, young lady."

"Aunt Kristen's mom is pretty young compared to her father." Heather knew this would get a reaction from her mother. It always had in the past.

"Not working this time, Heather," Emmy said.

"How much older? Let me see." Heather tapped her cheek. "Oh, yeah. Gracie told me there's an eighteen year difference. Who do I know that's eighteen years older than me?"

"I'm sure some of the crew members are in their thirties. You could flirt with them," Emmy said without betraying any emotion.

Heather stood up and cringed. "Like I really want to hang around with old men. I'm going to watch a movie."

"You could read a book. Your laptop is loaded with books," Emmy suggested.

Emmy ran into Ryan Lederer before Thursday's show in Birmingham, Alabama, with time to talk before soundchecks.

"How are the guys treating you, Ryan? Are they giving you a hard time?" Emmy asked while they waited backstage.

"It's not like the old days, Emmy. Everyone is more mature now. Do your guys still tease you?"

"Only Bobby. Everyone else treats me like their mother. It makes me feel so old."

Ryan laughed and asked, "Have you seen any recent photos of Emmy Rose?"

"No! Do you have some?" she asked. "I still can't believe you named your daughter after me."

"Em, I have a great aunt that I've never met. We named Emmy after her," Ryan teased.

"Nice try, but Jennifer told me the truth. How old is she now?"

Ryan pulled up some recent photos on his phone. "She turned five in May. You sent a card."

"I try to send cards, but I don't always remember how old everyone's kids are." Emmy stole Ryan's phone and looked through his photos. "She is adorable. I'm so glad she takes after Jennifer and not you."

"Your girls are the spitting image of you," he replied.

"Does Emmy Rose have an accent like you and Jennifer?"

"Not at all," Ryan answered. "She sounds like she's Australian. British accent, old man. Cheerio and all that rubbish."

"That has to be the worst impression of a British accent I've ever heard," Emmy said using her fake British accent. She and Ryan continued to talk to each other using accents.

Heather and Isabella walked up to Emmy and Ryan and listened to them chatting away.

"Have they gone wacko already?" Isabella asked.

"Three days into the tour, and Mom thinks she's Princess Diana. It's going to be a crazy summer, Isa."

Chapter Twelve

"Where are you now?" Emmy asked.

Father James looked to his right and then his left. "It's hard to say. All I can see are cornfields."

"Very funny. You're still in Illinois then, huh?"

"Apparently. I haven't crossed the Mississippi. I do know I'm on I-55, and I went through Springfield."

"How's the traffic?"

He chuckled and said, "I passed a tractor a few minutes ago. First vehicle I've seen in hours."

"Don't be silly. Did you really pass a tractor on the Interstate?"

"It was on the frontage road. I know it's Monday afternoon and didn't expect much traffic, but this is ridiculous. A state trooper pulled me over a while ago."

"Why?"

"He was bored and wanted to talk to someone. He claimed I was the first car he'd seen in three days."

"Why did I ever fall for your weird sense of humor?" she asked. "Did you stop by the house before you left?" Emmy asked.

"I did, and Carson was working in the yard. He showed me the list you left. Emmy, he's only staying for the summer. The list you gave him would take an army of men several years to complete."

"No it wouldn't. We didn't want him to get bored," Emmy said. She held up a finger as Nelson approached. "He didn't have any friends over, did he?"

"I saw no evidence of wild parties. There was the usual collection of beer bottles, drugs, naked women and..."

"Ha! Ha! I trust Carson. He's more of a loner than a party animal. I have to go. Nelson is waiting. I have to do a radio interview."

"How are the kids coping? You said Heather was bored after two hours on the road."

"She's adjusted. She and Deveron Esposito teamed up to form a band. They write silly songs together and play for the crew.

Isa and Kevin play this game called No Clues for hours at a time. Say hi to your parents for me. We will be in Kansas sometime in August. Maybe we can see them."

"I'll let them know. I'm sure they'd be up for a rock concert. Stay safe."

"You too."

Father James soon crossed the Mississippi River and entered Missouri on his way to Topeka, Kansas, to see his adoptive parents.

"I'm bored. When are we going to do something exciting?" Benjamin Bertucci whined to his father. "Kevin is gone for the whole summer. He gets to ride in a bus and have fun. I'm stuck here with nothing to do."

Tony listened to his son complain and said, "Would you like to take a trip out West?"

"I'd go anywhere at this point."

"Tell you what. I have four weeks of vacation to use. Let me talk to your mother, and maybe we can plan a trip."

"Make it soon because I'm going to die of boredom," Ben said as he trudged out of the room.

"What was Ben complaining about?" Sloane Bertucci asked. "I just passed him in the kitchen, and he was acting like he'd lost his best friend."

"He's bored because Kevin's gone."

"You should do something with the kids."

"I was thinking about something," Tony said. He got up and put his hands on his wife's shoulders. "What would you think about renting a motorhome and going out West. Colorado, Utah and maybe Arizona. We haven't been there for years, and I think the kids are old enough to enjoy it."

"Sounds like a good idea. Have you thought about what Mama would like to do?"

"She would probably like to stay home and enjoy the peace and quiet."

"Who would like some peace and quiet?" Mama Bertucci asked.

Tony's mother, who everyone called Mama, lived in her own section of the house behind the kitchen. She treated all the kids in the neighborhood as grandchildren.

"I was thinking about taking a vacation and going out West. I thought you would enjoy having the house to yourself. It would give you some peace and quiet."

Mama shook her head. "I'd much rather go on vacation with you. I would miss the children too much."

"Really?" Sloane asked. "Wouldn't they drive you nuts?"

"I thrive on the chaos," Mama said as three of the kids raced through the kitchen and out the door.

Father James turned onto the block where his parents lived. He saw one of the neighbors mowing his yard and waved. He pulled into the concrete driveway and noticed a new flowerbed in front of the porch. He parked, got out and stretched his legs. He smiled as his parents walked out the front door.

"We didn't expect you for another hour, son. Were you driving too fast?" Helen Boyanov asked.

Father James walked up the steps and hugged his eighty-seven year old adoptive parents. "I had the cruise set on seventy, and people were flying past me. How are you feeling, Dad?"

Josef Boyanov grunted. "I would feel a lot better if your mother would let me eat more food that I like. She makes me eat salads and fiber just because my doctor claims I need to stay away from fatty food. What does he know!?" Josef threw his hands in the air as he vented with his still strong Russian accent. Even after many years living in Kansas, both Josef and Helen often spoke Russian in their home. They lived in an area with many immigrants of Russian descent.

"Are you hungry? I have some soup on the stove. You need to eat. You look too thin, Mickel," his mother said.

"I told Emmy I would grow fat if I stay with you for more than a few days," Mickel said in Russian. "I can smell the soup from here." He patted his stomach and followed them into the kitchen.

"How is your little sister? Is she still so tiny that a wind off

110

the prairie would carry her miles away?" she asked still speaking Russian.

"Don't tell her I said so, but I think she's gained five pounds from the last time you saw her."

Josef laughed from deep in his ample belly. "Are you still afraid of the tiny one you call Emmy?"

"She can be as ferocious as a bear protecting her cubs," Mickel said as he sniffed the traditional Russian cabbage soup.

"I called the RV place," Tony said wrapping his arms around Sloane's waist.

"What did they say?" She moved his hands up and continued browning the hamburger. "I'm making taco salad because Coby requested it. Did you tell him to ask for it?"

"I might have mentioned we haven't had any for a while."

"Do they have anything available?"

"Remember the class C I told you about?"

"Vaguely. Refresh my memory," Sloane said. She added half of the taco seasoning envelope to the hamburger. "What is a class C?"

Tony explained the different types of motorhomes.

"This one has enough room for all of us."

"Including Mama? She wants to go, you know?"

"All nine of us. It might be tight quarters for the boys, but they won't mind. We could even bring a tent to let them sleep outdoors."

"How much?" Sloane asked.

"Too much, but we haven't taken a family vacation for so long. Let's not worry about the cost, okay?"

"Did you already make the reservation?"

Tony shook his head. "I told them I would call them back after I got your approval."

"Does it come with everything we would need?"

"Yes, and they offered to show me how to use everything."

Sloane looked at him and sighed. "You better call them back before someone else reserves it."

"What would you like to do today, Mickel?" his mother asked Wednesday after breakfast.

Mickel patted his stomach. "I can't do anything for an hour because I need to let my food digest. You made enough to feed the army."

Helen waved a wooden spatula at him.

"Actually, I would like to go past the store. Would you like to go with me, Papa?"

Josef looked at Helen and then their son. "I will go with you, but it isn't the same anymore."

Mickel drove to Grant Avenue where his father's hardware store was located.

"Isn't this the block were it is?" Mickel asked as he drove past the block for a second time.

"It is gone. They tore it down last winter and replaced it with another of those hideous strip malls. Now instead of a fine hardware store, you can buy Mexican food, get a tattoo and do your laundry. They call it progress."

"I didn't know this," Mickel said.

"It is of no matter," Josef said with a wave. "No one was going to operate another hardware store after I sold the building to that company."

"Why do you have to leave?" Helen asked. "You should stay longer so I can fatten you up."

"I would stay, but I have to be back for Sunday. I am still a priest and have responsibilities."

"Then I will fix a basket for you to take with," she said and headed to the kitchen.

"Papa, you must promise to let me know if either of you need my help. You aren't getting any younger," Mickel said holding his father's shoulders and feeling more bones than muscle.

"We are fine, and we have plenty of friends to help us."

Within an hour Father James was back on the road headed for South Hampshire. He stayed overnight outside of Quincy, Illinois. By two o'clock he was back in SoHam. Emmy called an hour later.

"I took the scenic route home. I could have stayed on the interstate, but it goes down to St. Louis and that adds miles. I took my time and enjoyed seeing more than you can from the main highway."

"Why didn't you drive straight through?"

"Because I'm not as young as I once was. I split the trip in half and stayed at a decent place just across the river."

"How are they doing?" Emmy asked.

"Papa has lost weight which is a concern because my mother makes enough food for the army."

"Did she try to fatten you up?" Emmy asked with a giggle.

"Yes, and she sent home a basket of food. She still thinks I can't cook."

"You can't! All you can do is throw food in the microwave. Will you stop by the house and check on Carson for us, please?"

"I will, but I'm sure he's okay."

Tony parked the motorhome in front of the garage and smiled as the entire family rushed out to see it.

"It's so big," Mama said. "How can you drive it?"

"It's not much different than driving my truck."

"Who will watch the house while we are away?"

"Kristen said she and Zach would guard the house and take care of Scout," Tony answered. "I thought about taking Scout with us, but Sloane said she is too old to travel. Scout I mean not Sloane."

Ben, Taylor and Coby raced inside to choose their bunks.

"Did they show you how to fill the water tank?" Sloane asked.

"Yes, and I know how to connect the electricity and the sewer pipe," he answered. "It's called the black water tank."

"What is, Daddy?" Noemi asked.

"That's where all the... stuff goes from the toilets. There are two, by the way."

"Yuck! That's gross!" Noemi said with a shudder.

Ben jumped out of the motorhome and announced, "I found a room for me and Taylor and Coby. It's way in the back and it has

113

three bunk beds. We're going to make it our fort and no one else can be in there."

Mama, Sloane and the older kids, Peter, Dotty and Noemi, followed Tony inside. Mama learned the motorhome had a full kitchen.

"It's too small for two cooks, so I will volunteer to do all the cooking."

"There's an outside kitchen, too," Tony said. "One cook can be working inside and the other outside."

After a quick tour, Dotty and Noemi confronted Tony.

"Where are we supposed to sleep? I assume you and Mom will take the bedroom."

"I thought you would sleep up there." He pointed to the area above the cab of the motorhome.

"That's a bed, too?" Ben hollered. "Can we make that into the enemy fort?"

"No! One fort is enough," Sloane said.

After a short discussion, the sleeping arrangements were finalized. Tony and Peter loaded the groceries. Tony made a final inspection and they headed to Colorado.

"Is this going to be like the Griswold vacation?" Dotty asked. "Are we Cousin Eddie and his family?"

"I did pack an ugly sweater," Tony replied.

Chapter Thirteen

The Prevost coach slowly made its way up the winding driveway. Kevin, Heather and Isabella sat with their eyes glued to the window aching for the first sight of home in a month.

"I can see the roof!" Kevin hollered. "The first thing I'm gonna do is jump into the pool."

The coach drew closer and it wasn't until it rounded a final turn that the house came clearly into view.

"I can't wait to sleep in my own bed tonight," Isabella said. "I might go to bed early, so I can spend more time snuggling up under the covers." She looked at her sister and asked, "Who are you texting?"

"Deveron. I invited him to come over and go swimming in the morning," Heather answered while keeping an eye open for their mother.

"Did you ask Mom?"

"I'll ask her if Dev can come. If I say he's on his way, she won't be as likely to say no."

The driver braked to a stop, and the coach settled into its lowest position. He opened the door and the kids dashed out.

"We're home!" Kevin ran toward the back deck flailing his arms over his head.

Heather and Isabella disappeared inside the garage. Carson stepped aside to avoid them and smiled as he stepped out into the bright sunshine.

"Hi, Aunt Emmy. I saw a blur... two blurs actually... race inside. Are you glad to be home?" He turned toward the back of the house as he heard a loud whooping noise. "Did you get attacked by Indians? I mean Native Americans."

Emmy laughed as she listened to her son getting rid of some pent up energy. "Can you tell Kevin's glad to be home?"

"How has the trip been so far?" Carson asked.

"Oh, the tour has been going great. The venues are smaller than in the past, but the crowds have been enthusiastic," Emmy answered. "The kids are finding ways to fight the boredom." She looked around the area south of the wide driveway in front of the garage. "I see you've cleared a lot of the brush already."

"It wasn't that hard. I used the chainsaw a couple times. Caden helped some, and Peter did until they left for Colorado."

"I heard about the motorhome. Noemi texted the girls and sent photos."

"Is it okay if I sleep at home tonight?"

"Of course, Carson. I'll tell Kenny to pay you."

He waved a hand. "That's okay, Aunt Emmy. It can wait until tomorrow, or even the end of summer. That way I won't spend any of it."

Kenny helped the driver unload the luggage they would need for the two nights they would be home. Tomorrow night fans would fill the SoHam Memorial Stadium for the annual Fourth of July Fridays At Five show.

"Daddy, can we talk to you, please?" Heather asked.

Kenny handed his newest guitar, a 1963 Gibson ES-330T, to Frankie Hanna, his longtime guitar tech, and grinned at his daughter. "Yes, Heather. What can I do for you?"

"Mom said it was okay with her, but that I would have to ask you and Uncle Andy first."

"What's okay with your mother?"

"Dev and I want to play three songs on the main stage after the doors open. We've been rehearsing all month."

"Hmmmm. Three songs, huh?"

"Yes, and you only have to pay us scale."

Kenny's eyebrows shot up. "Scale, huh?" He rubbed the three-day-old growth of beard on his jaw. "How do I know you're worth scale? Are you members of the local musicians union?"

"Daddy! I'm just a kid, but you and Mom are members. Please! Can we play?"

"It's all right with me if you get written permission from the band management." He paused and asked, "Do you have a manager?"

"Kevin said he would be our manager, but I told him to suck an egg. I'm not giving him a percentage. I got the booking on my own."

116

Kenny struggled but managed to keep a straight face.

"If Uncle Andy agrees, we can do it, right?"

"Yes, if he consents, I will agree."

Heather and Deveron raced away to find Andy Walker, the only manager in the history of Fridays At Five. He was known for his toughness with promoters who dared stray from their contracts in even the smallest way.

"There he is?" Heather shouted. She led Deveron through the maze of people. "Uncle Andy! Uncle Andy! I need to talk to you."

He turned and saw Heather sprinting toward him. "Slow down, Heather. You might run over someone."

"Uncle Andy, I need your permission for something that Mom and Daddy have already approved, but I need your consent before we can actually do it, so could you please say yes or else I will just die?" she asked faster than ordinary people could talk.

"If I caught all that, you are asking for permission to do something that needs my approval. Is that right?"

Deveron nodded.

"That's it," Heather said. "Will you say yes?"

"Could you be more specific with the details because I have no idea what you are asking?"

Heather explained her plan to the last detail.

Andy shrugged his shoulders and rolled his head to ease some unseen tension in his neck. "So, Frankie will bring out your guitar, set up two mics and you are going to sing three original songs. Correct?"

Heather's nods matched Deveron's and even surpassed his in intensity.

"And you're asking for scale."

"Yes."

Andy glanced at Ty Dalicandro, who had been listening.

"I've heard them rehearsing, and they have talent," Ty said. "This could be history in the making. The world debut of... does your act have a name?"

"We want to be called The Heather and Deveron Band."

"Do you have backing musicians?" Ty asked.

117

"It's just us, Mr. Dalicandro. At least for tonight," Deveron answered. "Bobby said he might play drums for us if we get another gig."

"Well! This is most unexpected, and never in my career as a band manager have I allowed an unknown artist to appear uninvited on the stage of any artist I have represented."

Heather's face showed her crushed hopes as clearly as a window to her soul.

Andy's face slowly evolved from a scowl to a smile. "In this case, I will make an exception. Ty, make sure my new artist has the full support of the entire Fridays At Five organization. Give her anything she requests."

Heather's smile warmed his heart as she hugged him hard enough to cause him pain.

"Your heart is as hard as a marshmallow over a bonfire," Ty said.

The doors to the stadium opened and thirty minutes later Lexi Gabriel, the program manager for SoHam radio station WSHO, walked to the middle of the stage to welcome the crowd. She did the usual promo announcements and then looked behind her. She watched as four crew members quickly set up a keyboard, acoustic guitar and two microphones.

"We're ready," one of the crew members said into a walkie-talkie and exited the stage.

Andy Walker strode to the stage and Lexi handed him the microphone. "Before I bring out those other bands, I want to introduce a band making their worldwide debut. Please give your full attention," Andy said as if issuing a command to his army, "to the Heather and Deveron band!"

Frankie Hanna, who was nearly as famous as the guys in the band, led Heather and Deveron to center stage. He adjusted the mic for Heather and made sure Deveron's guitar was plugged in.

"Thank you, Frankie," Heather said smiling at her father's shy, first cousin.

"My pleasure, sweetheart. Knock 'em dead!" Frankie said with a grin.

"Hello, we are the Heather and Deveron Band..."

118

Kenny and Emmy watched from behind a wall of gear at the side of the stage.

"I think we've created a monster," Kenny whispered. "She will have the crowd wrapped around her finger after one verse."

"She's been paying attention to her father and mother for years," Andy said as he watched with pride.

Emmy bit her lip to keep from crying as Heather sang her original songs.

"We have one cover we'd like to do if we have time," Heather looked to the side of the stage where Ty Dalicandro and Nelson Grapella stood.

Ty smiled and Nelson gave her a thumb-up. He waved toward someone standing behind the backline and turned around to watch Emmy and Kenny.

The crowd erupted as Jeff Rawlings, Jeremy Lenhart and P.J. Joseph walked out on stage. Dave Persching waited as a riser with a four-piece drumset was quickly rolled into place. He took his seat behind the kit, smacked his sticks together and the chords of "Sweet Girl" thundered across the open stadium.

"This is a thank you to Mom for putting up with my bad attitude on this trip. I love you, Mommy," Heather said and seamlessly started singing the lyrics.

Kenny put his hands on Emmy's shoulders and felt the sobs flowing through her body.

"How are you gonna follow that?" Andy Walker said trying in vain to hide his tears.

Heather sang the last notes of one of the first songs her father ever wrote, handed the mic to Frankie, who had appeared almost magically, and raced toward her mother.

Emmy's arms were open wide as Heather collided into them almost sending them both crashing to the floor of the stage.

"I love you even more," Emmy said softly.

Kenny met the guys backstage and asked, "Who set this up? Even Andy didn't know about the encore, and did your doctor give you permission to play today?"

Jeff grinned and answered, "I didn't ask for permission."

Dave handed his drumsticks to Deveron. "I set it up. We

heard the kids practicing and heard Heather explaining how she was sorry for her attitude and wanted to apologize to Emmy. I thought this would be better than a private apology. Did Emmy say anything?"

"She was kinda speechless for a moment, but she whispered something to Heather. I couldn't hear what she said, but they were both crying."

"We would like to do one more for you if you'd like," Emmy said ninety minutes later.

The crowd's roar signaled their approval.

Emmy looked to the side of the stage and waved. Heather and Isabella joined her.

"I asked my darling daughters to join me on this one. They actually came up with the harmonies for it. You might have heard it. It's a tribute to a dear friend who departed this life too soon."

The crowd roared, but quickly a silence filtered over the stadium as Emmy said, "This is called 'Gideon's Heart.'"

"That was a perfect way to end your set," Nelson said as Emmy left the stage with tears flowing down her cheeks.

Emmy accepted a tissue from Susan Lemmert and after drying her tears said, "I wanted to open with 'Yolanda's Song' because it was kinda the beginning to my career and close with 'Gideon's Heart' to end my career. I can't see myself ever being on this stage again."

"I understand, Emmy, but I hope you realize how much those people love you, and how much your music has meant to them."

"I know how they feel, but it's time, Nelson." Emmy hugged him and headed to her dressing room with a heart filled with love and peace.

Chapter Fourteen

"Is this supposed to be a surprise party for Mom?" Kevin asked as he joined his sisters, father and several members of both bands in the catering room backstage in Denver's Mission Palace. "I might have told her happy birthday accidentally."

"It's not a surprise party," Isabella said. "Mom said she didn't want a fuss, so we are having cake and ice cream without any presents."

"Is she sad because she's getting so old?"

"Kevin Michael! Your mother is not getting old," Kenny said sternly. "She's only thirty-nine, and you will learn that is far from being old when you get to that age."

"If he survives that long," Heather said with a frown.

"If who survives that long? Emmy asked as she and Bobby O'Connor entered the room. "Did I miss something?"

"Kevin thinks you're sad because you are so old," Heather said.

"Squealer!" Kevin shook his fist at Heather then said to his mother, "I didn't mean you're old like Grandma or those old ladies at church who have to use walkers to get around. Some of them have got to be close to a hundred, but I don't think of you as that old, Mom."

"Thank you so much, Kevin. I do think I can walk without the aid of a cane."

"Should we sing now?" Isabella asked.

Kenny started and everyone sang to Emmy.

"Shoot! We forgot to light the candles," Kevin said.

"No matter," Andy replied. "It might start a forest fire if we light that many candles."

Emmy stuck out her tongue. "Kevin might not be the only one who needs to worry about his survival."

"Are we gonna have a surprise party for Mom next year when she turns forty?" Kevin asked his father later.

"It might be difficult to surprise her next year. She will be expecting something."

"Maybe we could surprise her by not surprising her."

"That makes sense in a weird kind of way, Kevin," Kenny said.

"Everyone has to help clean the motorhome," Sloane insisted as the kids scrambled to exit their home for the previous month. "Mama and I are not cleaning up your messes."

Tony shut down the class C rental and turned to Peter. "I'm used to driving this rig now. I think we might need to buy one of our own. It will be cheaper in the long run if we use it enough."

"You might want to clear that with Mom," Peter replied. "She has been complaining her back hurts from the cheap mattress."

"If we had our own rig, we could buy a better mattress. Will you help unload the luggage? I don't think the boys are going to be much use for a while."

"Sure, Dad."

Ben raced upstairs and called Zach. "We're home and I have a thousand pictures to show you. Get over here now!"

Noemi texted Grace and then Natalie Hammond. Dotty called her closest friends. Coby used his mother's iPad and tried to FaceTime Grayson Hammond.

"I will try to find him," Liz said. "I know he's around here somewhere."

Soon all the friends knew the Bertuccis were home.

Zach raced through the woods that separated his home from the Bertucci home next door.

"I have to help clean up the beast, but then I can show you my pictures."

"I'll help," Zach offered.

Soon the 'beast' was clean and passed Sloane's inspection. Tony would return it and get an Uber home.

"We turned the bunkhouse into a fort," Ben explained. "No girls were allowed in."

"Did you get scared in the mountains? I've heard there are bears and mountain lions all over Colorado and Utah."

"We didn't see any bears or lions, but I saw tons of deer and elk and these goats that would climb the cliffs."

"In Colorado?" Zach asked.

"I think that was either in Montana or Idaho. Dad drove us all over the place."

"Did he get lost?"

Ben shook his head. "No because the beast had special navigation. It showed the roads with bridges that were too low."

"It would have been fun to get stuck under a bridge," Taylor said.

"Where are those pictures from?" Zach asked handing Ben's phone back.

"I think that's Zion National Park in Utah. It was cool, but there were way too many people, and we had to park in town and take a shuttle to the park. This is Arches. I liked it better. Oh! I gotta tell you what we did one day."

"What did you do?"

"We were in Moab and Dad lined up this Jeep tour for all us guys. We took some dirt roads and sometimes we were on the edge of a sheer cliff. It had to be like hundreds or maybe thousands of feet to the bottom." Ben extended his arms to emphasize the height or depth of the cliffs. "Sometimes we could see the river at the bottom, but other times it was too far down to see it. We had to cross little rivers at times and go up the steep banks. Once we had to back up because another Jeep was on the trail. That was scary!"

"I don't like cliffs," Zach admitted.

"Dad doesn't either, but he tried not to show it. I remember Aunt Emmy telling a story about how Dad got scared when they were on vacation somewhere in Utah a long time ago. Aunt Emmy used to tease him about it."

Taylor added to Ben's story. "We had to squeeze through this one place where you could almost touch the walls of this canyon from inside the Jeep. It was so narrow. Then we had to go down this super steep section and under this humongous boulder that was kinda blocking the road."

"Yeah, but the coolest place was called the Shafer Trail. It started at the top of Canyonlands and went down these switchbacks to the bottom of the canyon. From the top they looked like they went straight down, but once we were on them, it wasn't so bad."

"Were there steep cliffs?" Zach asked.

"Sure, but the road was wide enough for the Jeep to go. We didn't pass any other Jeeps going down it. When we got close to Moab and the river, we passed these walls with old pictures carved into the cliffs. They were halfway up the sheer cliff."

"How did they get there?"

Ben and Taylor shrugged.

"Don't know unless the natives were giants."

"Did you see the Grand Canyon? I want to go there someday."

"Don't bother, Zach." Ben waved his hands.

"Yeah, there were like millions of tourists all over the place. Most of them were foreigners, and they all had cameras," Taylor said.

"Is it real steep?"

"It's so massive and deep that you can't see the bottom," Ben said.

Taylor added, "It's supposed to be like eighteen miles across in some places and probably five or ten miles deep."

"Dad joked that they should build a bridge across it."

"What did the girls do while the guys were having all the fun?" Zach asked.

"Dunno, but Mom and Dotty and Noemi went horseback riding one day while we were hiking through some canyons," Ben answered. "I want to go back someday when I can drive. I want to drive a Jeep on some of the real bumpy trails. At night!"

"Cool! That would be awesome," Taylor said. "I want to do the White Rim road and camp by the river."

"Where's that?" Zach asked.

Ben flipped through some photos until he found the one he wanted. "It's near Moab. Part of the time it's just a boring dirt and gravel trail, but then it gets real close to the edge. See this?"

Zach looked closely. "It doesn't look like much."

Ben and Taylor laughed

"What?"

"It's hard to tell, but that edge drops straight down over a thousand feet. Boom!" Ben clapped his hands together. "If you take one wrong step, or if the Jeep slips just a little... It's all over! No need to search for a body. There are probably hundreds of skeletons at the bottom."

Is anyone hungry?" Mama hollered up the stairs. "I made sandwiches and we have potato salad."

"You hungry, Zach?"

"Always."

The boys ran to the stairs. Ben and Taylor scrambled down the stairs like a herd of elephants. Zach took his time and stayed in the center of the staircase.

"Since I don't have to go back to work until Monday, I thought I would look for a class C of our own," Tony said while eating breakfast the next morning. "Do you think we should buy one or just rent them as needed?"

Sloane added salt to her scrambled eggs, took a bite, slowly chewed it before answering, "You enjoyed driving that thing more than I would have thought possible."

"I know it would be a large investment, but we could save money if we take family vacations every year. It could even be used on weekends and holidays to take short trips."

She added more salt. "Are you thinking a new one or used?"

Tony smacked the bottle of the glass bottle to force the resisting ketchup out. "New would be nice, but I've read the depreciation can be quite a lot. It might be better to look for a used one. We wouldn't take the hit, and any problems should have been fixed."

"Just looking, right?"

"I'm not going to make a rash decision based on one vacation. We might not need a rig that large. Peter will be going to college soon, and Mama might not want to spend another month in that tight of a space."

"The kitchen was too small for two cooks," Sloane said. "It won't hurt to look."

"There's a place in New Linden that sells new and used Winnebagos and Airstreams. I could start there."

"It was fun to camp out without having to sleep in a tent like the boys."

"They wanted me to stay with them, but I told Ben I couldn't leave you alone because you would get scared."

"Did he buy it?" Sloane asked with a grin.

"No, he said I was afraid I'd hurt my back."

Tony returned in time for dinner with several brochures and a better idea of what might suit their needs.

"Sloane, would you mind if I run up to Newcastle? There's a RV place up there that sells new and used rigs," Tony asked.

"So it's a rig now," Sloane teased.

"I need to talk the lingo if I want to sound intelligent."

"Didn't you promise the boys you'd spend today with them? They look forward to Saturday's so much," Sloane reminded him.

"They're still sleeping. I could run up there with Peter and be back before they get up."

Sloane sighed and said, "Okay, but just looking, right?"

"I'm still looking. I don't know what floor plan or what kind of rig to buy yet. There are so many choices."

Tony and Peter returned four hours later. Tony set a handful of brochures on the countertop and shook his head. "I'm more confused than ever."

"Are you talking about RVs or just confused in general?" Sloane asked with a smile.

"Both," Tony admitted with a grin. "I should have taken you with."

"Why is that?"

"Some of the units have thin mattresses and others have comfy ones."

Sloane shook her head and walked away.

Chapter Fifteen

For years the extended Kimmerle and Lindower families had been meeting in the small port town of Drewsey Bay, Maine, to spend their summer vacations. The families owned a large two-story house and three rustic cottages at the edge of the woods on the north side of the quaint, former fishing village. In the late seventies tourism replaced fishing as the main source of income for the five hundred or so people who called Drewsey Bay home. This year Pastor Tyler Hammond hesitated to take his annual family vacation to Maine because of what he had described to his associate pastor Wyatt Pearson as a plateau in the church's growth.

Wyatt found Tyler in the church office Saturday afternoon staring at his laptop. "Why aren't you packing? You're supposed to leave after church."

"I've been looking for cheap flights from Portland to Chicago, but they don't exist."

"I thought you were driving the Sienna. Am I wrong?"

"We are driving, but I thought if I could find a cheap flight back and forth, I wouldn't have to miss any Sundays."

Wyatt shook his head at his close friend. "Is your ego so inflated you think the church cannot survive two weeks without you."

Tyler chuckled because he knew Wyatt was trying to push his buttons. "Yes, that's exactly right. My ego will not allow me to imagine the possibility of a church service without me."

"I thought your head looked bigger for some reason."

Tyler ran a hand through his hair. "I need a haircut and haven't had time to stop at Louie's to get one. I might start cutting it myself."

"That's a great idea. You could give yourself a Mohawk like Jarrett Bindley," Wyatt teased. "You are aware there are other barber shops in Crest Ridge and SoHam, right?"

"Yes, but I like Louie's. It may take longer, but I get to meet different people every time. And my ego is kept in check by the Tuesday morning Bible study group. They take delight in critiquing my sermons before we start the study. I've actually picked up some good tips from the seasoned members of the church."

"I know you sense the church is at a plateau right now, but you have earned your vacation time. You might find it beneficial to take the time away and recharge your batteries. Even that rabbit cartoon character eventually runs out of juice."

Tyler closed his laptop. "Point taken. I am leaving the church in capable hands. I will check my emails once a day, so I'm not totally out of the loop."

"Are you ready for the trip?" Kristen Randolph asked Liz Hammond after church.

"I just have to dash home and throw a few things in the van. Otherwise, we are ready to hit the road."

Kristen looked around the now empty foyer.

"Are you waiting for Wyatt?" Liz asked.

"Yes, I am making lunch for us while the kids are playing next door."

"I take it things are progressing nicely between you and Wyatt. Not that it's any of my business," Liz added.

"It has, and I don't have any secrets from you," Kristen said with a sigh. "Zach and Wyatt are getting along so much better now. Gracie has always been fond of him."

"I'm so happy for you."

"I heard Tony is taking care of Derby while you are gone. Is that true?" Kristen asked to change the subject.

"Yes, normally we leave her with the Burns family, but they're going away, too," Liz answered. "We've taken Derby over there before, and she and Scout get along great. They love to run through the woods."

"How do the kids handle the long trip? How many hours does it usually take? You might have told me, but I have forgotten."

"It's over a thousand miles to Drewsey Bay, and we could get there in eighteen hours according to Mapquest, but that would be driving without stopping."

"That's a long drive," Kristen said. "Zach and Gracie would

stage a mutiny if suggested such a trip."

"We used to do it overnight when Natty and Grayson were babies. Now we make extra stops. David will turn three while we're in Maine."

"I can't believe he will be three already. I still think of him as a baby."

"I know! They grow up so fast. Phoebe will be six in December," Liz said.

"She is so smart. I heard her reading in class, and you have obviously taught her well."

Liz smiled and said, "That girl loves to read. Natty and Grayson handle the trip pretty well now. They have their iPads and keep busy. Phoebe and David get on each other's nerves at times."

"How do you handle that?"

"The easiest way I've found is to have the boys sit together in the back. Grayson is very patient with his little brother, and Natty and Phoebe are best pals."

"Zach and Gracie get along okay, but they have their own friends."

Tyler and Wyatt approached.

"Are you ready to lock up?" Liz asked.

"I just need to grab my study Bible from the office and I will be ready. Where are the kids?" Tyler asked.

"In the van. Phoebe is ready to get underway so she can see Bumpa."

"She loves her Bumpa," Kristen said. "She was telling everyone in Sunday School how he is going to take her fishing for lobsters."

Liz laughed. "We always go out for fresh lobster while we're there. The restaurant has a tank, and you pick out the lobster you want. She's always done that with Bumpa, and she calls it fishing. She can be such a goof at times," Liz added sweetly.

"I heard Tyler mention to Tony that going to Maine has been a family tradition for years. Why Maine? It is so far away."

"Dad grew up in Maine as did his father and grandfather. Mom's family was originally from there, and she has a sister who still lives in Drewsey Bay."

Kristen and Liz walked outside and headed for the Sienna and Kristen's Acura RDX while Tyler and Wyatt locked the church.

Liz continued, "His grandfather was a doctor and was the first Lawrence Dustin Kimmerle."

"The first?" Kristen asked.

"Yes, my father's name is actually Lawrence Dustin Kimmerle III."

"Everyone calls him Dusty though."

"The first one was known as Lawrence. Then his son, who was the second Lawrence Dustin, went by L.D. Dad goes by Dusty and my brother Larry, who is Lawrence Dustin IV, is just called Larry. If he has a son he will have to name him Lawrence Dustin V."

Kristen's mouth dropped as Liz explained. "I've never heard of anyone being the fifth anything, or the fourth for that matter."

Liz shrugged and said, "I think it's more common in Maine. He and Allie were hoping for a boy when they had Maggie."

"You have a great vacation. We will be praying for a safe journey, and I know Wyatt will do a great job while Pastor Tyler is away."

"The police have arrived, Pastor Wyatt," Ellis Smalling said.

"I will talk to them first, Ellis," Wyatt replied.

"They will want to talk to me, won't they?" Smalling asked. "I'm the head usher, and it was my responsibility to place the money in the safe. This is all my fault."

Wyatt placed an arm around the elderly man's thin shoulders. "No one is blaming you. You were distracted by the commotion."

"Hello, I'm Officer Galbraith." The young officer held out his identification. "I hear there's been a break-in."

Wyatt led Officer Galbraith to the church office.

"Someone broke the glass and unlocked the door. The morning's offering was sitting on this counter."

"Is that normal?" the officer asked.

130

Wyatt shook his head slightly. "It's usually placed in the safe to be counted later."

Officer Galbraith took notes as he asked questions and Wyatt answered.

"Mr. Smalling is our head usher. He is the one who places the offering in the safe, but he was distracted by an argument between two teen boys and accidentally left it on the counter."

"And it wasn't until after church was dismissed that anyone noticed the broken glass, correct?"

"Yes. Normally the church treasurer and two other members of the finance committee would count the money, however Mrs. Burns is on vacation."

"Were the two teenagers members of your church?"

"They were visitors, I believe, but it's possible some of the teens might have known them," Wyatt said.

Officer Galbraith looked at the walls and ceilings of the area. "No security cameras?"

Wyatt shook his head. "We haven't found them to be needed."

"Until now," Officer Galbraith added. "I will make a report and some tech people will arrive soon..."

Wyatt shook hands with Officer Galbraith later, returned inside and walked up to Mr. Smalling.

"I will resign my post," Mr. Smalling said. "This was all my fault."

"Mr. Smalling, your resignation will not be accepted. I have already talked to Pastor Tyler and he told me emphatically you are not to feel guilty about this. You have been a faithful and esteemed member of this church for over forty years. Your service has been invaluable, and we are positive it will be for years to come."

After talking to Officer Galbraith Thursday morning, Wyatt called Tyler in Maine.

"So Braden Reynolds invited them to church, huh?" Tyler asked.

"Yes, he knew them from school, but both Officer

131

Galbraith and I are certain Braden knew nothing of their plans. Braden feels as guilty as Mr. Smalling."

"And they have been arrested and charged?"

Wyatt laughed and answered, "They were foolish enough to keep all the checks and admitted to spending the cash on drugs. This was not their first offense, and this time they might have to spend time in jail."

"I feel bad for Braden and Mr. Smalling, and I know God will use this for good somehow."

"Do you feel this would not have happened had you been here?" Wyatt asked.

Tyler laughed and answered, "No. I have learned my lesson. This would have happened no matter where I was. I think you've handled the situation better than I might have."

"I don't suppose we'll ever know how much cash was taken."

"No, and I know God will provide whatever we need."

"I'm so glad to be sleeping in my own bed tonight," Phoebe said as Liz turned off the bedroom light. "I love seeing Bumpa and all my cousins and everybody, but I missed my church friends."

"Two weeks is a long time for you to be away from home, huh?"

"I forgot how many days there are in a week," Phoebe said pulling her blanket up.

"You will see many of them tomorrow night. Wednesday is Family Night, and you can tell all your friends about fishing for lobsters and learning how to water ski."

Chapter Sixteen

Emmy joined Kenny on the couch in the bus lounge as they left St. Louis heading for home. The summer tour ended on August 30 as planned. Though the crowds were smaller than previous tours, by cutting back on expenses, the band was able to turn a profit.

"Are the kids asleep?" Kenny asked.

"They are in bed," Emmy answered. "They might not be asleep yet, but they are settled down. Kevin is really anxious to get home. He wants to tell Ben and Taylor all about the tour."

"I feel tired," Kenny admitted. "It's been a while since we packed so many shows into just three months."

"Do you guys think you'll keep touring even if you play smaller venues?" Emmy asked.

"As long as we can stay in the black, we will. There are so many people who depend on us to tour for their own financial security. We've had to let a lot of the part-time employees go, but we still have a dedicated team." He put an arm around her and whispered, "Do you still feel the same?"

"Yes, I haven't changed my mind. Unless something drastic happens like the world economy collapses and we need the money, tonight was my final concert."

"You are still going to sing at church, right?"

"Yes, I'm not giving that up."

"Will you join me on the road and sing with me?"

"No way! My days traveling in a smelly bus with you and the guys are over for good. I am now a full-time writer."

"Would you consider writing lyrics with me?"

"I might do that, but you have to pay me," she insisted.

"And how much would you charge? Would it be thousands of dollars?"

She grinned and said, "It might be thousands, but instead of dollars, I was thinking more along these lines." She kissed him deeply and for much longer than he expected.

"Thousands, huh?" he asked.

"I value those a lot more than dollar bills."

"I might have a few thousand left," he said as he pulled her onto his lap.

"Kenny, did you talk to Ryan Lederer before he left for Knoxville?" Dave Persching asked Sunday evening. "Jeff told me he definitely won't be joining us on the road until the summer of 2020 at the earliest."

"I thanked Ryan for doing a great job this summer, and told him the details of our offer."

"What did he say? Did he jump at the chance to join us?"

"Actually, he thought about it for a day and called me back. He said he appreciated the offer, but his place is in Knoxville with his family. He thanked us for the generous salary offer, but family comes first."

"Do you know what he plans to do?"

"He mentioned looking for a job as a teacher. He does have a teaching certificate but not the experience."

"I can understand that. I lost my family partly because of placing the band and the money we earn above them. I'm glad Ryan has more sense than me."

"We don't need to make a decision right away, but we need to think about who else we might want to hire in case we do a small tour in the fall or after the new year. I like the idea of doing smaller, shorter tours as long as we aren't losing money."

"I agree. I don't want to be that band without any concern for the people behind the scenes. There are too many people depending on us for their livelihood. As long as we enjoy making music. I want to keep touring on whatever level makes sense."

"Kenny, can you think of anyone else we should invite?"

"Who all did you invite?" Kenny asked as he slipped into bed beside her. They had decided a week before they got home from the tour to have a Labor Day cookout at the house.

"I invited all our Bristol Ridge friends and family. Everyone will be here except Andy. He left to visit his brother. The Robertsons are still in town, so they can make it. Your parents are coming."

"What about Tony?"

"I invited Sloane and the kids, but I told Tony he wasn't welcome," she said.

"Yeah, right."

"I told him he had to help with the grill. Brady and Diane will be here. Of course I invited Kristen and Wyatt. I think he's planning to come."

"Did you invite anyone from church?" Kenny asked turning off his light.

"Liz and Tyler. Oh, I heard from Lynette and Paul. They are coming and bringing the girls. Her twins are going to be sophomores at Olivet. I told Rory, but he and Rochelle have to work. Hospitals don't close down for holidays."

They continued talking about who might come to the cookout for several minutes.

"So, your best guess who be a max of fifty or sixty people, huh?" Kenny asked.

"Yeah, but some of the people from church already had plans, so I doubt if they make it. I checked and we have enough water and pop in the garage fridge. Since the weather's good, I told the kids they could use the pool. I told Tony he and Peter would have to be the lifeguards. Did you remember to bring more picnic tables up to the deck?"

"I did. I had Bobby help. We used his truck and moved them. I found one in the woods that wasn't worth moving. It's mostly rotted away. We might need to replace a couple of them."

"I'm glad we have such a large deck. I love having everyone over to eat together."

"You're really making Tony earn his steak, huh? He has to man the grill and the pool."

"Oh, I guess I could ask Pastor Tyler to help Peter. He's a good swimmer."

"Did you finish the list? I want to run to the store early before it gets too busy."

"It's on the island. If you think of anything else, go ahead and buy it. Just don't buy any mustard. We have three bottles in the pantry."

135

"Is Mama making the potato salad?"

"Of course, and she's making baked beans, too. She insisted."

"Good. Hers are the best," Kenny said turning onto his side away from Emmy.

"Hey!"

"What?" he said without moving."

"Don't I get a good night kiss?"

"Have you written any lyrics for me?" he asked turning over and grinning.

"I might need some inspiration," she replied.

"I'm not paying for inspirations. I need actual lyrics."

"How about this?" She sang the words to one of her early songs.

"Not bad. I suppose that's worth a little kiss."

"That was more than a little kiss," she said later with a sigh.

"Did you already go to the store?" Emmy asked the next morning as Kenny carried two bags of groceries into the kitchen.

"I did, and there are more bags in the Odyssey. I bought more water and pop was on sale, so I picked up five cases. If nobody drinks it, that should last the rest of the year."

"I'm glad our kids drink more water than pop," Emmy said emptying the groceries. She held up a box of mostaccioli. "Why?"

"I thought we were out."

"There are two boxes... oh, never mind. We will use it eventually."

Tony and Peter arrived at noon and saw Kenny on the rear deck by the grills.

"I'm reporting for duty," Tony said with a mock salute. "Where is the general?"

Kenny closed one of the grills and pointed to the house. "She's in the kitchen making taco salad. People are supposed to supply their own meat, but we have extra hot dogs, burgers and a few steaks just in case."

"Aunt Emmy asked me to watch the pool," Peter said. "I recruited Carson to help. Is that all right?"

"Sure, Pastor Tyler is going to help, too."

By one o'clock most of the expected guests had arrived. Emmy, Sloane and Mama were using the kids to run all the food to the deck. Tony and Father James kept the grills busy making sure everyone had enough meat. They even made room for grilled corn on the cob.

"I think everything is ready," Emmy said at one thirty. Pastor Tyler, would you offer thanks, so the kids can eat. I'm sure they're all starving."

Tyler prayed and Emmy gave instructions about getting in line for food.

"Kevin! Save some beans for other people," Heather shouted.

"It's all right," Mama said. "I have two more pans in the oven. I know how much the boys like to eat."

Emmy waited until all the guests were eating before filling her plate. She looked around and saw an empty chair next to Liz.

"Miss Emmy, sit with us," Phoebe said.

Emmy sat down beside her. "Are you ready for school to start tomorrow?"

"I wish I could be in Mommy's class," Phoebe answered.

Emmy looked at Liz.

"We are concerned she might be bored in kindergarten. She's already reading at a second grade level, but according to the state regulations, she was too young to start kindergarten last fall."

"Heather and Isa got bored with kindergarten, but they were born in January, so there was no way they could have started school any earlier."

Kevin tapped his mother's shoulder and asked, "Mom, can we go swimming now? We're through eating."

"Would you wait until either Peter or Carson can watch the pool. I don't want anyone swimming yet."

"Okay, but we can go as soon as Peter's ready, right?"

"Yes. Did you eat something besides baked beans?" Emmy asked.

"Mom! I ate two hot dogs and some potato salad. You can ask Ben or Grayson. They saw what I ate."

"Okay, but if some of the girls want to use the pool, you have to let them. You can't say it's just for boys."

By three o'clock the leftovers were put away, the pool was full of kids and the adults were sitting in groups on the deck to talk. Emmy was talking to Kenny's mom and Mama Bertucci about the recipe for baked beans and baked corn casserole when she saw Wyatt leading Zach and Grace to the table where Kristen was sitting with Sloane, Liz and Lynette.

"Could I have everyone's attention for just a moment?" Wyatt asked after Zach and Grace took a seat by their mother.

All eyes turned to him as he stood at the end of the table next to Kristen, Zach and Grace.

"What is he doing?" Emmy asked Kenny's mom.

When Wyatt took a knee, Emmy gasped.

"Kristen Randolph, would you and Zach and Grace do me the honor of becoming my family? I love you all and want to spend the rest of my life with you."

"Holy crap!" Emmy said too loudly.

"Hush," Mama scolded.

Emmy watched Kristen put a hand to her cheek and nod several times. "Yes! Yes, I will marry you. We will marry you." She stood up. Wyatt kissed her and they hugged tightly. Zach and Grace joined the hug.

"Mama, did you know about this?" Emmy asked. "You used to know beforehand when anyone was getting engaged."

"I had no inkling of this, Emmy, but I dare say I'm happy for her. Her new man appears to be deeply in love with her."

"He's a widower, right?" Elly Colwell asked.

"His first wife passed away several years ago," Emmy said. "I have to go hug Krissy if I can pry her away from Wyatt."

After letting the newly engaged couple have a moment of privacy, everyone closed in around them. The men shook hands with Wyatt, except for Tyler, who uncharacteristically gave him a hug, and the women congratulated Kristen. Emmy finally had her turn. She hugged Kristen so hard Liz had to remind her to let Kristen breathe. Emmy looked at Kristen's hand.

"Where's the ring?"

Wyatt heard this and reached into his pocket. He pulled out a small jewel box. "Sorry! I forgot. I've only proposed once before." He opened the box and pulled out a ring. "It's nothing fancy and we can buy one you like better, but I wanted to have something to show I was serious." He placed the ring on her finger, and Kristen's tears flowed like the Shoshone Falls in the spring.

"This one is perfect, Wyatt," Kristen said. She kissed him without shyness even with all eyes upon her.

"Did I miss something?" Tony asked. "I was answering a call."

Emmy poked him in the side hard enough to hurt him and her hand. "TMI, and Wyatt just proposed to your favorite cousin, you doofus."

"What? When? Why?"

"Wyatt proposed just now, and he did it because he loves Krissy and the kids." She smacked him again using her other hand.

Tony shook hands with Wyatt and turned to Kristen. He didn't attempt to fight back tears as he gave her a hug and lifted her off her feet.

Later, the leftovers were brought out for the people who were hungry again.

Emmy sat with Kristen, Liz and Sloane and talked about school for a time.

"When are you gonna get married?" Emmy asked out of left field.

"Em, they just got engaged two hours ago," Sloane said. "It takes time to plan a wedding."

"Kenny proposed on Sunday, October 27 at halftime of a Bears/Vikings game, and we got married on April 5 at 1:22 in the afternoon. We didn't have a long engagement."

"How can you remember all those details," Liz asked.

Emmy shrugged and said, "Those were kinda important events in my life."

Kristen looked at the ring again, sighed and said, "I don't know how Wyatt feels, but I don't want a long engagement. I would like to be a family before Christmas."

Emmy giggled and Liz nudged her.

"We've heard the stories from Kristen about why you didn't want a long engagement," Liz said.

Emmy bit her lip. "I was pretty bad wasn't I?" She asked Kristen.

"You were horrible to live with. You about drove me insane talking about how you couldn't wait..."

"Don't you dare say I couldn't wait to have sex," Emmy said.

The ladies laughed and Sloane said, "She didn't have to, Emmy. You said it yourself."

Chapter Seventeen

"Mom! You don't have to come inside," Heather said. "We are in eighth grade. We know where to go. You will embarrass us if you treat us like babies."

"Fine! I won't hold your hands and walk you inside," Emmy said sarcastically.

"I don't need any help either," Kevin said. "I know what room is mine, and there's Ben. I want to talk to him. See you after school." He waved and raced away.

Emmy sat in her BMW and watched. *They wanted me to hold their hands just a couple years ago. Was I like that at their age?* She closed her eyes and tried to remember eighth grade at Adolph Tockstein Junior High. *I suppose my friends and I acted like we were something special because we were the oldest kids in the school. I hope Isa doesn't develop an attitude. She's always been sweeter than Heather.*

Tony knocked on her window interrupting her thoughts. She rolled down the window.

"You okay?" he asked.

"Yeah, the kids didn't want me to walk inside with them. I feel old."

"I hear ya. Carson and Peter caught the bus to St. Raymond's. I dropped Dotty off at Barclay and then brought the rest of the tribe here. I should get a job as an Uber driver."

"Did you go inside?"

Tony chuckled and said, "Coby let me walk with him. He's in third grade, so next year he will be too old to have me walk him to class." He shrugged and added, "Face it, brat. We are getting old."

"Hush, you dork, and don't you dare say something stupid like I'll be a grandmother in a few years."

"Wouldn't dream of it," Tony checked his phone for the time. I'm off to Liberty Manufacturing. Have to earn my dollar-a-day."

"They pay you that much? I'm surprised you don't have to pay them." She stuck out her tongue added, "Hey! Did you take those two steaks home yesterday? I was going to use them for dinner tonight."

"I grilled them. I get to eat them."

"Well, at least you let some of the guests eat what they brought. See you later."

Shortly before ten the members of the original 'The Only Hope' band met in Kenny's basement family room. They were reuniting to record a third CD and the first since disbanding in 2010.

"Who's missing?" Kenny asked. He turned when the door opened and Bobby O'Connor entered out of breath.

"Sorry I'm late, but the traffic was horrible." He plopped onto the couch, leaned back and crossed his legs. "Did I miss anything?"

"How could you be late?" Boyd Goldman asked. He pointed toward the guesthouse. "I can hit a golf ball and land it in your yard."

"Did I say traffic? I meant Shay was feeling sick."

"Yeah, if you want to use that for an excuse, I guess we'll let it slide," Adam said.

Though Adam Vicini was now a member of Fridays At Five, he was the original keyboard player and lead singer for 'The Only Hope'. Since Fridays At Five was idle at the moment, he was recruited to resume his old position.

Kenny got their attention. "Stuart, Bruce and I listened to the demos and I think we have some strong songs to work with. Since the studio isn't booked for anything else right now, we can take as much time as we need."

Everyone turned as Emmy entered.

"I can't believe you guys want to record a new CD without me. Don't you love me anymore? I was your first singer."

"If you want to be absolutely accurate," Perry Johnstone, one of the original guitar players, said, "we were actually your backing band."

"Semantics," Emmy said with a wave. "Just wanted to let you know I'm available if you need a good singer."

142

Bobby snickered and Emmy was going to attack him until Kenny grabbed her around the waist.

She settled on sticking out her tongue and saying, "You guys look so much older now than when we first hit the road."

"Em," Kenny cautioned.

"We are older, Emmy," Boyd said, "but that means you are older, too."

Bobby looked around. "In fact, Mrs. Colwell, you are older than any of us, except Kenny, and he was never in our band." Bobby pointed to Mason Williams, who was replacing Sean DelSasso, who had replaced Ryan Lederer, and said, "Except for Mason, I'm the youngest one here."

"That's true, Bobby," Adam replied.

"Yeah, and you're still a punk," Emmy teased.

They took a few minutes to talk about the early days of the band.

Emmy looked up at Perry and asked, "Were you always this tall and skinny?"

He laughed and nodded. "I haven't shrunk or grown an inch since I last saw you."

"Do you have a new girlfriend?" Emmy asked drawing laughter from everyone.

"Same ol' Emmy," Bobby said. "She always had to know about everyone's love life."

Boyd raised a hand. "I have a new girlfriend, too, Emmy. I met her in church, so you might like her."

"Good. I won't bother you anymore."

The guys worked on a couple new songs until two in the afternoon. They took a break and Emmy came downstairs.

"I'm gonna pick up the kids soon. How's the recording going?"

Adam handed her a lyric sheet. "We're stuck on the second verse. Got any brilliant ideas?"

Emmy read through the lyrics, tilted her head, tapped her chin for a few seconds and said, "How about this?" She sang two lines.

"That works!" Adam said.

"Thanks, Emmy," Boyd added. "Do we have to give you writing credit?"

"My attorneys will be in touch," she teased. She kissed Kenny and headed for the stairs. She stopped and said, "Oh, I saw the list of titles you were thinking of using. I have a different suggestion."

"What might that be?" Bobby asked.

"Inhabitants," she answered and ran up the stairs.

The guys looked at each other.

"Inhabitants," Adam repeated a few times.

"It fits the theme of the tunes," Boyd said.

"I like it," Perry added.

The guys looked at Mason.

He shrugged and replied, "Hey! I'm the new guy. I'll go along with whatever."

Adam laughed and said, "I suppose she'll want credit as the producer now."

Riordan and Sadie Schulenberg enjoyed the luxury of having enough volunteers to have four teams of musicians for the worship service. One of the teams being comprised of teens and a few college-age students. Each team was scheduled to be on the platform one Sunday a month. Because of work schedules and other availability issues, some volunteers did double duty. Emmy drove the girls to worship band rehearsal Thursday evening. The teen band was holding auditions and Heather and Isabella were now old enough to try out.

"Mommy, I'm nervous about tonight," Isabella admitted on the way to church.

"You don't need to be nervous, Isa," Emmy said glancing over her shoulder into the backseat. "You've sung on stage with me numerous times."

"That's different," Isabella said.

"How?"

"Mom!" Heather exclaimed. "Singing with you is different. It's fun and no one expects us to sing on key or anything. To your audience we're still cute little girls. The Schulenbergs will actually listen to make sure we have talent and know what we're doing."

"You have talent. You inherited it from me," Emmy said with a grin.

"I thought we got it from Daddy," Isabella replied.

"I helped a little, and you know how to sing on key. You know how to harmonize. The teen band should consider itself fortunate to have you as part of the group," she said, "and besides, you are both as cute and pretty as could be."

"Mom!" both girls said simultaneously.

"It's important to have talent, but it doesn't hurt to look pretty."

"Are you going upstairs with us?" Heather asked. "We're supposed to have tryouts in the Cross Fire room, and you might make us nervous if you're there."

"I will be in the new sanctuary with the adult team. I'm not scheduled this week, but I won't be a distraction there."

"Thanks, Mom," Heather said.

Emmy parked and walked inside with the girls.

"See you later," Isabella hollered as she and Heather raced upstairs.

Emmy watched them for a moment then headed to the back of the new sanctuary to the music suite. She saw Rebecca and Ryan Deighton going over a new song and walked up to them.

"Hi, Emmy, I didn't know you would be here," Rebecca said.

"I brought the girls to the teen tryouts. They didn't want me to hang out with them, so I thought I'd join you guys. Who's watching Isaiah?"

"He's in the nursery," Rebecca answered. "I'm glad you're here. Riordan and Sadie are upstairs with the teens tonight. They asked me to lead the rehearsal, and we could use another singer."

"I'm going to be here, so I can help if you want."

Mason Williams walked up behind Emmy. "What are you doing here, Mrs. Colwell?"

"I brought the twins, and why did you call me that?"

"Emmy, do you make your band call you Mrs. Colwell?" Robby Collins asked.

145

Robby, a drummer, and his wife Regina, who sang, had been part of the worship team for years. They were actually in charge of worship for a time.

"You know I don't, Robby," Emmy said. "Mason is teasing me. When he first joined my band, he was quiet and never said a word unless we asked him a question. But after being on tour with Bobby O'Connor all summer, now he likes to tease me."

Rebecca kept quiet while studying the features of the two men. Robby was stockier and resembled a bodybuilder while Mason was taller and more slender.

"Are you familiar with the songs on the list for this week?" Rebecca asked.

Ryan chuckled and said, "She might know this one."

"Why is that?" Emmy asked.

"Well, because you wrote it," he answered.

"Oh," Emmy said feeling embarrassed.

The girls finished trying out for the teen group and waited in the sanctuary while the adults finished rehearsing.

Emmy joined them and asked, "How did it go? Are you part of the team?"

"Mrs. Schulenberg said we could sing the lead parts most of the time. Either she doesn't know anything about singers, or she thinks we have talent."

"I think she's a wise judge of talent, Heather," Emmy replied.

Emmy saw the girls in the family room Friday after school. "Is your homework finished?"

"Mine is," Isabella looked up from her book and answered.

Emmy looked at Heather and repeated the question.

"I'll do it later, Mom. It's the weekend, and I have to text my friends first. I'll get to the homework whenever."

"Heather Rose! You know the rules. Homework before fun."

"But this is important. Some of the girls from school are trying to organize a slumber party for tomorrow. I need to know where and when."

"Young lady, you need to do your homework first, and you need to ask permission to go to a party. Either do your homework, or give me your phone." Emmy held out her hand.

"No! I'm not giving up my phone, and I'll do the homework later. It's Friday night."

Emmy walked up to Heather and tried to grab the phone. Heather jerked it back, then got up, ran past Emmy and raced upstairs. Emmy heard her door slam, sighed, and looked at Isabella.

"My homework is done, Mommy, and my phone is in my room."

"Thank you for not giving me a headache, Isa."

Emmy went up to Heather's room and knocked.

"Go away, Mom! I'm not giving you my phone."

Emmy tried the door, but it was locked. "Open the door now, Heather."

"No! I'm busy."

"Do I have to talk to your father?"

"You do if you want a successful marriage," Heather said not meaning to be sarcastic.

Despite her anger, Emmy grinned as she walked away. *Well, she was telling the truth.*

By the time she told Kenny, her anger had subsided.

"I will talk to her," he said.

"Now, please."

Kenny went upstairs and knocked. "It's Daddy. Can I come in?"

Heather opened the door and handed him her phone. "Can I have it back as soon as my homework is done?"

"I suppose so, but you should apologize to your mother. It wasn't very respectful to yell the way you did."

"I'm sorry, but Mom doesn't understand how important it is to have friends."

"Your mother was once your age. She knows more than you realize."

"That was eons ago. Life as a teen is more complicated now. We have to face peer pressure like you wouldn't believe.

147

Even from kids at church. You may not believe it, but all the teens who claim to be good Christians don't always make good choices."

Kenny stared at Heather for a moment and then down at the phone after she closed her door. "I think this is a job for Emmy or some other lady to handle."

Heather finished her homework, came downstairs and apologized to her mother and father.

"Is this because of... you know?" Emmy asked.

"Mom! I don't care to talk about that in front of Daddy," Heather whispered.

"You may have your phone back, but you are not going to any slumber party this weekend. Is that clear?"

"Yes," Heather answered without revealing the slumber party had been quashed.

"Who's taking me to football practice?" Ben asked Saturday morning. "I need to be there by nine."

"I'll do it," Peter said.

"No way. You don't have your permit yet," Sloane told him. "I'll take you, Ben, since your father has to work today. I don't know why he has to fly to Pittsburgh for these HR department meetings."

"Can I go with?" Peter asked.

"You can go, but I'm not letting you drive around the parking lot like your father did."

"That was at the church when there weren't any cars around, and he made sure I was going slow."

After school Tuesday afternoon Isabella noticed a new book on the kitchen island. She picked it up and carried it into the family room where Emmy was sitting.

"When did this come out?"

"Oh, it was just released. Do you like the cover?"

"It's okay. It looks like an old-fashioned formal dance."

"It's supposed to be a dance from the late nineties. Does it really look old-fashioned?" Emmy asked taking the book from Isabella.

"Well, *The Sweetheart Ball* is not exactly a great title. The clothes are obviously out of fashion and the decorations look so lame. I didn't know you were finished with it. It didn't take nearly as long as the last one."

"It was easier to write, Isa."

Isabella grinned and asked, "Is that because there isn't any sex in it?"

Emmy blushed and stammered, "That's not the entire reason."

"Is this one of those books we aren't allowed to read until we're older?"

"You can read it now. You are old enough to understand it."

"Do you mean because of... you know?"

"Not entirely. You are mature enough to understand more than I did at your age."

"Can I ask you something without you telling Daddy or Heather?"

"Can I tell Kevin?" Emmy asked patting a spot on the couch next to her.

"I'll die if you tell him."

"I was teasing. I would never tell your brother anything that would embarrass you."

Isabella sat beside Emmy and whispered, "Will I always get cramps before it comes? Will it always hurt so much?"

"Why didn't you tell me it was hurting, sweetie?"

"I didn't want to talk about it."

"You can always talk to me about anything. I will always listen. In fact, I could give you something that I use for pain. You could try that, and if it doesn't help, we could always see my new doctor. She's really nice, and knows how to talk to young girls."

Chapter Eighteen

"Did he get it?" Sloane asked as Tony walked into their bedroom.

"He did," Tony answered. "Can you believe Peter's old enough to get his driver's permit? It wasn't all that long ago when he started kindergarten." Tony sat on the edge of the bed, sighed and stared at the wall.

Sloane watched for a time then sat beside him and nudged his shoulder with hers. "Are you thinking about her?"

"Who?"

"You know who I mean."

Tony took a deep breath. "It's hard to believe Heather's been gone for so long."

"It happened only a few months after we were married. That was in 2005 in case you can't remember."

"I remember." He patted her thigh. "Peter was only two when he came to live with us."

"Yes, and Dotty was one. She was still a bit wobbly on her feet and learning how to talk. Now they are both in high school, and Peter will be driving a car."

They heard someone rushing up the stairs and down the hall.

"Hey, Mom! Did you hear?" Peter shouted knocking on the doorframe and holding up an important document. "This came in the mail today."

"I did. Congratulations, son. We are so proud of you," Sloane said as her voice cracked.

Peter rushed to the bed and sat beside her. "Are you guys okay? You seem sad."

"We are happy for you and sad at the same time."

Peter gently wiped a tear from his mother's cheek. "You were thinking about my first mom, right? It's not October yet. Why were you thinking about her?"

Tony cleared his throat and stood up. "We think about Heather more than just in October."

"I know. I think about her sometimes, too. Once in a

while... Maybe every couple of years or so... Dotty will ask Mama about her. Mama will try to think of something new to tell us, but often it's a story we've heard before."

"She would be very proud of you and Dotty," Sloane said giving Peter a squeeze. "We are so proud of you, too."

"Does that mean I can take the truck for a drive. Maybe just around Bristol Ridge for now?"

Tony laughed and said, "Your mother said we are proud of you. She didn't say we've lost our minds."

"If I have to, I could drive the Sienna."

"Maybe we can do that later, okay?"

"Sure, Dad. I need to text Carson and let him know I got it. That might inspire him to get his before it's too late."

Emmy stomped into the house, tossed her purse and keys at the desk, turned around, pointed a finger at Heather and Isabella and shouted, "In the library this instant. You are going to listen to me without any of the back talk or attitude. Do you understand? I am tired of your sass and rudeness."

"But Mom!"

Isabella pulled her sister down the hall toward the seldom used library. "Heather, just chill. This isn't the time to fight back. Mom caught you being rude to that teacher's aide."

They entered the library in the corner of the house across from the family room, sat on the leather couch and waited.

Heather pulled out her phone and started texting.

"I would put that away if you want to keep it. I haven't heard Mom this angry since Kevin Michael swore at Ben and Taylor."

"It wasn't all my fault," Heather protested. "That aide said I should stop trying to stick my nose where it shouldn't be. Then she said 'that might be impossible because it's so big' and laughed."

"She was joking. You don't have a big nose."

Heather grinned. "We look alike so if I have a big nose, so do you."

The door burst open hard enough to bang against the wall. Emmy slammed it shut and marched into the room. She stood in front of the girls with hands on her hips and fire coming from her eyes.

"It..."

"Not a word, Heather Rose! I heard what you said and that was the last straw. Hand over your phone."

Heather looked at her phone and surrendered it.

"Yours, too, Isa."

Isabella surrendered her phone without a word.

"I know you might not be as guilty as your sister, but your attitude has been less than satisfactory lately."

Both girls stared at the floor.

"I heard part of what the aide said, and she used poor judgment talking to you in that way, but that doesn't give you the right to disrespect her like that."

Heather looked up at her mother and rolled her eyes.

"Don't even," Emmy said.

"Didn't you ever get mad at your mom or at some stupid teacher's aide?" Heather asked.

"Yes, but that doesn't mean I was right. One of the commandments is to honor..."

"We know them, Mom."

Isabella nudged her sister.

Emmy silently counted to ten then sat in one of the recliners facing the couch.

"Sorry, Mom," Heather said. "That was rude."

"You are a few months older than I was when I was in eighth grade, but the circumstances are similar. My friends and I thought we were the rulers of the school because we were the 'high and mighty eighth graders' and could do whatever we pleased." Emmy used the air quotes that always made the girls cringe because of the lameness. "I made some poor choices for friends that year. I did some things I came to regret later." Emmy paused and closed her eyes.

Heather looked at Isabella out of the corner of her eye. Isabella responded with an elbow to Heather's ribs.

Emmy opened her eyes and continued, "I would hang out with these kids after school because my parents would be at work.

152

They would be drinking, and I've told you before how I would drink some of Daddy's beer even though I didn't like the taste. I was at least smart enough not to smoke like they did. I finally came to my senses and stopped hanging out with that crowd when two of the boys robbed a convenience store."

"Mom, we've heard this before," Heather said. "We aren't going to be like you. We know better than to do that kind of stuff."

"I hope not, but I worry about you. At least you're going to a Christian school, but there are still temptations."

"Things are totally different now, Mom."

"Things are worse in many ways. You have access to material that would never have been dreamed of when I was thirteen."

"If you mean pornography and stuff like that, you don't need to worry. One of the teachers caught two boys looking at pictures, and we think it's disgusting."

"There are others evils. Violence is everywhere. Your brother used to play those war games on his phone and every week there seems to be a shooting at some school. I don't want to even think about the movies where there is so much violence and sex."

"What are we supposed to do?" Isabella asked.

"Are we supposed to hide in our rooms and read the Bible all day?" Heather asked. "Sorry, I didn't mean it like that. I read the Bible and try to learn from it."

"No, we aren't supposed to hide in a closet," Emmy said. "We are supposed to be the light in a world of darkness. We should let the love of Jesus shine through us. That means we love other people no matter what they might do or say to us. We don't fight cruel words with more cruel words. That isn't what He taught us to do."

"Do I have to apologize to that aide?" Heather asked.

"I can't tell you what you have to do. You need to listen to the Holy Spirit and let Him guide you."

Heather sighed and said, "I felt guilty about it as soon as I yelled at her. Even though she said some mean things to me, I shouldn't have responded like I did."

"When you see her, maybe you can tell her that."

153

"Are you going to keep my phone forever?" Heather asked.

"No, but you will need to earn it back."

"How long do we have to behave before we get them back?"

"It's not a matter of behavior change, Heather. You have to change your heart and your attitude. It's what's on the inside that matters to God."

"We messed up, didn't we, Mommy?" Isabella asked.

"Yes, but God will forgive you. He forgave me for all the times I messed up."

Emmy opened her arms and the girls stood up to get hugs.

"I love you both so much," Emmy whispered.

"Even when we make mistakes?"

"Yes, Isa, even then."

"How did your week at work go, Kristen?" Emmy asked Saturday morning. Did you have time in the evenings to work on the wedding?"

"No, I didn't think about the wedding. By the time I got home from work, I was exhausted. Totally worn out mentally."

"I could come over and help. I'm not doing anything," Emmy offered.

Kristen thought about it for a moment. "Okay, but you better not try to talk me into a huge wedding. Wyatt and I want it to be small and intimate."

"You have to wait for the intimate part," Emmy teased.

"Promise?"

"Fine! I promise not to try to persuade you to invite a thousand people or to tease you about sex."

"Don't make promises you cannot keep."

Emmy went to Kristen's house, and they worked on wedding plans until dinnertime.

"You know it doesn't matter how many people you invite, Krissy. The church will hold close to a thousand people," Emmy said.

Kristen shook her head. "I do not want the reception to be at the Lincoln Hotel like yours. Wyatt and I want it to be at the

154

church. We don't want a huge catered dinner. Just something simple."

"You can't dance at the church."

"We are aware it would be frowned upon," Kristen said. "Will you help with the invitations? I want to make sure they get mailed in time."

"Of course I'll help. Did you tell them at work you are going to take time off?"

"Yes, Em, I have plenty of vacation time coming."

Kenny called a family meeting later that month. Emmy and the kids marched into the family room and sat in front of the fireplace. Kenny stood in front of the fireplace looking quite serious. His forehead was furrowed and his eyes concentrated on the ceiling.

"Why do we always sit over here to have these meetings?" Kevin asked

"Because you can't see the TV from here," Kenny said.

"We can't see it anyway because it's turned off."

"Well, I like sitting by the fireplace."

Kevin sighed and crossed his arms over his chest. Emmy put her arms around the girls.

"What are we supposed to talk about?" Kevin asked.

"I'm glad you asked," Kenny said as he paced in front of the fireplace.

The girls and Emmy giggled.

Emmy whispered, "Let him be a dork for a while. At least he's not wearing an ugly sweater."

"I want to discuss touring. Specifically, the direction future Fridays At Five touring should take. Your mother has decided not to go on the road for the foreseeable future and I fully support her decision. However!" He raised a hand and stopped pacing. "I must continue to earn a living to support my family."

Heather and Emmy yawned when he wasn't looking.

"You are old enough now to have some say in the matter. I'm referring to the timing of the tours. It's often more profitable to tour in the summer, but touring at other times of the year can be just as important. However, I have to consider your education. We need to choose which high school you will attend and how much that will cost. Then there is college to think of."

Heather raised a hand and Kenny saw it after a few seconds.

"Yes."

"I would like to attend Olivet if I may."

"Yes, maybe we have some time to make that decision." He looked at Emmy and asked, "Am I being a total dork?"

"Maybe ninety-five percent, Dad," Kevin said.

"I'm sorry, but I have been concerned about how our touring affects my family. I don't have a typical job that allows me to be home every night."

"You're home all the time when you aren't touring. That kinda evens things out," Kevin said.

"We understand why you have to go on tours," Heather said. "It's still kinda cool to have a rock star for a father. Even if your music is old-fashioned."

"Thanks, I think."

Emmy raised a hand.

"Em, you aren't in school."

"Andy called me a few days ago to say he might need back surgery next year, and he is going to retire from traveling with the band. Does that effect your plans?"

"He will turn sixty next March, and he should be able to stay home if he wants."

"Can I take over his job?" Kevin asked. "I like how he yells at people."

"He doesn't do that nearly as much these days," Kenny said. "Andy has people in place to take up the slack. You will have to wait a few years to take over, Kevin. Sorry."

"By that time your band will be as old as the Stones," Emmy said.

"I can't get no respect," Kenny said.

"I think you mean satisfaction, dear," Emmy said.

Kenny shook his head as everyone giggled.

Chapter Nineteen

After praying and leading a devotion study to open the October board meeting, Pastor Tyler held up an envelope. "Most of you will not be surprised by this. It's a letter of resignation from the Schulenbergs. They have felt God calling them back to California, and Riordan has accepted the position of senior pastor of the Lamanda Vista Nazarene Church. If you remember they are from Pasadena. The letter says they have enjoyed their time with us, and will miss everyone. Their final Sunday will be November 3." Tyler set the envelope on the table. "I didn't make copies, but you may read it if you desire."

"Does the fact Sadie is expecting play a part in their decision?" Tanya Paduchik asked.

"You would have to ask Sadie," Tyler said with a chuckle.

"Do you have any candidates to replace the Schulenbergs?" Roger Goldman asked.

"I do and I have scheduled a meeting with them Thursday afternoon before rehearsal."

Jim Rosek raised a hand. "May we ask who you have in mind?"

"No, Jim, it's top secret," Carol Wisnewski, the board secretary, teased.

"All righty then. My bad," Jim said raising both hands in surrender.

"I have two people in mind who would make excellent worship pastors. Since the technology department is separate now, and has been since Chase left, the role of worship pastor has been simplified."

"Drum role, please," LaShae Mabry, the newest and youngest member of the board, said providing her own sound effects.

"Emmy Colwell and Rebecca Deighton."

"Two excellent choices," Dylan Michaelis said.

"Let's hire them both," William Griffith proposed.

"Rebecca is expecting, but that is a temporary condition," Tyler said.

"Would she have the time considering she will have a baby and a toddler at home?" Marley Menconi asked.

"She would have to make that decision," Tyler said looking around the conference table. "She will have Ryan's help."

"Doesn't Mrs. Colwell travel quite a lot?" LaShae asked.

"Whoa! I'm not going there," Mr. Rosek said again holding his hands in the air.

Mr. Griffith looked at Mr. Michaelis and laughed.

"Should I strike that question from the minutes for LaShae's safety?" Mrs. Wisnewski asked with a straight face.

"What did I do? Why is everyone making fun of me?" LaShae asked trying to shrink into her chair.

Tyler chuckled and explained, "I think everyone is referring to you calling her Mrs. Colwell."

"That is her name, right?"

"Technically, it's Mrs. Colasanti-Colwell," Mrs. Wisnewski answered.

"I once heard Emmy get after one of the young ushers for calling her Mrs. Colwell. She told him that was her mother-in-law, and he should call her Emmy."

"I'm sorry. Please don't tell her what I said."

"We will protect your safety," Tyler said.

At that moment Tony Bertucci rushed in out of breath and took the only empty seat. All heads turned to him.

"I'm sorry to be late, but I got stuck at work. Did I miss anything?"

Mrs. Wisnewski pointed at LaShae while looking at her laptop and read, "Ms. Mabry referred to Emmy as Mrs. Colwell."

Tony slumped in his chair and sighed. "Oh, no. I pray she never hears about it."

"Sorry, Liz, but I got here as soon as I could. I had to wait for Ryan to get home from work," Rebecca Deighton said rushing into Pastor Tyler's office.

"We are still waiting for Tyler. He had to take a call from Mrs. Cordell. Her mother is back in St. Bart's."

"It's all right," I just arrived a few minutes ago," Emmy

158

said. She stood up and inspected the books in Tyler's floor-to-ceiling bookcase.

"If you are looking for some of your books, I have them at the house," Liz said with a grin. She wrapped some of her long blonde hair around a finger. "Natty wants to read *That's Not Possible, Is It?*, but I think she should wait."

"Oh, please don't let her read it yet. Sometimes I feel guilty for even writing about such a controversial subject."

Rebecca adjusted some of her long, black, wavy hair into a bun. "What is the book about?"

"Would you tell her, Liz?" Emmy asked.

"It's your book, Em. You know more about it than me."

Emmy took a deep breath and said, "My new series is about two sisters in high school. Claire and Ruby. Liz referred to the second one. The controversial subject is sex. My Ruby character loses her virginity in the book, and I wonder if it might influence young girls to feel that premarital sex is okay..."

"Sorry, I'm late, but I had to take a call," Tyler said as he sat behind his desk.

Emmy put a hand to her face. "Did you hear what we were talking about?"

"All I heard was something about premarital sex."

"Shoot me now," Emmy said trying to slide down the leather chair and disappear into the floor.

"Relax, Emmy. I told Tyler about the scene where it happens," Liz said. "I thought you did a great job of showing the tension in the scene, and letting the reader know you didn't approve of Ruby's decision. I loved the way you were in her head."

Rebecca fussed with her hair again to avoid the conversation.

"If we are finished with a critique of Emmy's book, I will tell you why we are here," Tyler said. "I read the Schulenberg's letter to the board Monday night, and I told them of my recommendations to fill the post." He looked at Rebecca then Emmy.

"Who? Not me," Emmy said. "I can't lead the worship team."

"Emmy, you've been doing it for years. You are a natural," Liz said.

"But Rebecca has a degree in Worship Arts, right?"

"Yes, I do, but I am expecting in early April. I will have my hands full."

"Emmy, you and Rebecca are my only options. Robby and Regina made it clear again they would not accept the position."

"I could help Rebecca," Emmy said.

"I could assist Emmy," Rebecca said simultaneously.

They looked at each other and laughed.

"I have an idea," Liz said. "Rebecca could take over the team until such time as she needs to step away. Emmy could take over until Rebecca is able to return. Or, they could be co-worship team leaders starting now."

"Emmy, do you think you and Rebecca could work together?" Tyler asked with a grin.

"She knows more about music than me," Emmy said.

"No, you are the professional," Rebecca replied.

Tyler looked at Liz and shrugged.

"Ladies, you are both extremely talented. You should take some time to pray about it. I'm sure God will provide an answer."

"Can we pray now?" Emmy asked.

"Certainly, we can all pray, and maybe this time the Holy Spirit will answer immediately."

Emmy giggled and said, "Kinda like Instant Messenger, huh?"

"I will start the prayer, and anyone can pray as they feel led."

Fifteen minutes later, the answer became apparent.

"So, you will be co-leaders of the team, but only Rebecca will be paid. Is that correct?"

Emmy and Rebecca replied, "Yes."

"I will leave it up to you to figure out how this arrangement will work best."

"Do we have to start right away?" Emmy asked.

"The Schulenbergs will be here for three more Sundays. You can take over then," Tyler said.

Emmy grinned and asked, "Is there money in the budget to remodel the music suite?"

Tyler sighed and answered, "You need to talk to Ralph and Bill. They are the heads of the finance and building and grounds teams."

Since 'The Only Hope' was taking three days off from recording, Kenny used Monday morning to visit the local Chrysler dealership on the border between SoHam and Crest Ridge. He had only briefly mentioned his plan to Emmy the previous evening.

"Where are we going?" Emmy asked. "And why do you have the title to your Acura?"

"I've been watching YouTube videos about going off-road, and I want to look at a Jeep."

"Why? There's nothing wrong with this car. It doesn't have 20,000 miles on it. It's like brand new. It still smells new."

"Yes, and it has quite a bit of equity."

"A Jeep, huh? Would you let me drive it?"

"Sure! I was thinking it would be perfect to drive through the woods around our house."

"You want to trade a perfectly good car in for a 4x4 to drive through the woods around our house. Is that it?"

Kenny shrugged and then nodded as he left Bristol Ridge.

"I have a better idea."

"What's that?"

"Let's head over to Mercy Hospital, and I'll see if Rory or Rochelle can get you admitted to the insane asylum."

"Em! I'm not crazy."

"Your opinion," she said rolling her eyes. "Have you ever driven a Jeep?"

"No, that's why I want to check one out. Take a test drive. It can't hurt to look, can it?"

"Just a test drive, right?"

He nodded.

Three hours later Kenny parked his new yellow Jeep Wrangler Unlimited Rubicon in the driveway outside the garage.

He turned it off and looked at Emmy.

"What?"

"You were the one who said 'just a test drive', remember?"

She grinned, opened her door and jumped down to the driveway. "You did have a lot of equity in your Acura."

"Why did you want a yellow one?"

"It stands out. You will be able to spot it so easily in a parking lot, and it was the only Rubicon with a heated steering wheel and the turbo engine."

"Do you think the kids will notice when they get home?" Kenny asked.

"Aren't you gonna let me take it to pick them up?"

"Seriously? You have to stay on the roads to get there. You can't take off through the woods."

"I know! I'll take it through the woods when we get home. We can sorta use the snowmobile trails and maybe even build some obstacles to crawl over."

Kenny shook his head. "I never should have let you watch that YouTube channel."

"Let's plan a trip out West like Tony took. We can figure out a time in our schedules that works."

"Should we take the kids with us?"

"Why not? Kevin would have a blast..."

"And the girls would be bored to death."

"What do you think of Emmy's new Jeep?" Kenny asked when Tony stopped by to pick up Ben and Taylor after school.

"It's not my Jeep," Emmy insisted. "You suggested it first."

"I like it. We rented a Wrangler and drove some of the trails around Moab."

Emmy laughed. "Ben said you got freaked out by the cliffs."

"Not all of them, brat," Tony admitted.

"It handles differently than a car or a crossover," Kenny said. "I could really tell it on the expressway."

"It takes a little getting used to. My truck rides better."

"Did Kevin tell Ben what I suggested?" Emmy asked.

"Maybe. What?"

"I want to make some off-road trails through the woods. We have enough space to do it."

"For a ATV or a side-by-side?"

"No! For the Jeep. We would have to widen some of the snowmobile trails."

"The Jeep's larger than you think, Em."

"It would be good practice for when we take a vacation to Moab."

"I've been looking for a motorhome for a while. Haven't found one that Sloane and I can agree on, but I saw a fifth-wheeler for sale that would work. I might have to trade in my F150 for something more heavy duty."

"Where would you put it?" Kenny asked. "You wouldn't leave it outside, would you?"

"I talked to Mr. Robertson about renting space in his museum."

"Is that what he's calling it?" Emmy asked. "Did you see my new car?"

"The old Packard?"

"Yeah! Isn't it awesome?"

"I saw it. Not sure if I'll fit."

"Who said you ever get to be in it?"

"Do we have to go home already?" Ben asked. "We want to help Aunt Emmy drive her Jeep through the woods. We found this huge boulder to drive over."

Emmy shrugged.

"Maybe another day," Tony said.

Tony took a personal Wednesday and spent several hours at Mike Ketelsen's RV Center in New Linden. He emailed Sloane the floor plan of a fifth wheel trailer by Grand Design. She called him back and they talked for twenty minutes.

"If you think it works, go ahead and buy it or lease it or whatever you do with those things," Sloane said.

"I want to trade the truck, too."

"Get whatever you need to haul the beast."

The kids were home from school when Tony parked the

163

truck and fifth wheel in the road. The younger boys raced down the driveway. Everyone else took their time.

"What do you think, guys?" Tony asked.

"It looks bigger than the beast we had before," Ben hollered. "Can we go inside?"

Tony opened the door. He watched as Sloane and Mama stared at his new rig. "Well, do you like it?"

"Why did you park in the street?" Mama asked.

"I wasn't sure I could turn it around by the garage, and I didn't want to back it down the driveway. I need more practice before I attempt that."

"Where are you going to put it?" Sloane asked. "You can't leave it here."

"Mr. Robertson agreed to let me store it in his building. He cleared out one side to give me plenty of room."

"You better not damage one of his cars with this monster," Sloane said.

Tony gave everyone a tour. Sloane and Mama were impressed by the large kitchen.

"I love the island and this is a real refrigerator," Mama said, "but I doubt I will take another camping trip. I need my own bed."

The younger boys declared the bunkhouse off limits to girls. Dotty and Noemi decided to let their mom and dad have the bedroom up front. Peter said he could sleep anywhere.

"We even have room to take Scout," Tony said.

Scout barked her approval.

"Can we camp out in the fifth wheel tonight, Dad?" Ben asked Saturday morning. "We need to make sure everything works."

Tony looked at Sloane. "Mr. Robertson said I could park it next to the building. He said there's water and electrical hookups and room to practice backing it up."

"Make sure you don't take advantage of his generosity."

"He said he might like to use it someday. I told him he could use it anytime he wants."

"Go ahead," Sloane said.

"All right!" Ben hollered. "Can I invite Zach and Kevin and Caden?"

"Sure," Tony said. "The more the merrier."

Sloane laughed and whispered to Mama, "I bet they're all home before midnight."

Tony practiced moving the fifth wheel around in the level area behind and to the west of Mr. Robertson's building. Mr. Robertson helped by being the spotter as Tony learned just how far he could turn the truck to backup the trailer. After an hour he parked it in a fairly level spot.

"It has an automatic leveling option. It's as easy as pushing a button," Tony said.

The trailer was close enough to connect to the water and electrical on the side of the building.

"All you need now is a dump station," Ben said.

"I don't think I'll be adding that anytime soon," Mr. Robertson said with a laugh.

"What should we have for dinner?" Tony asked later.

The six boys settled for hot dogs and beans.

Tony figured out how to use the cooktop and sent Ben and Taylor home for the food.

"Mom! You should have seen Dad driving the beast around. It was awesome. He didn't knock anything over and never ran into Grandpa Robertson's building."

Sloane shook her head and loaded up a cooler for the boys.

"It it warm enough?" Mama asked.

"Yeah, Grandpa Robertson and Dad figured out how to turn on the furnace. It's just like living in a real house except you can move it anywhere you want," Taylor said.

Ben asked, "Do we have to let Noemi and Heather and all the girls use it as a clubhouse? We want it to be just for boys."

"You have to share, and remember it will be inside the building most of the time. You can't pester Mr. Robertson and ask to go in there."

Ben's shoulders sagged. "Okay, I guess we'll have to use the fort we built last summer."

165

Chapter Twenty

"Before we go out for the first service, Sadie and I would like to thank all of you for your faithful service over the years," Riordan spoke to the worship team members in the music suite. Most of the musicians and singers had gathered to say goodbye to the Schulenbergs. Only a few were missing.

"It's hard to say goodbye," Sadie said holding a tissue. "This has been our home for five years. Jude was only two when we arrived, and now he's eight and I'm expecting his brother. I will hold a place in my heart for all of you."

Riordan took time to shake every man's hand. The ladies gathered around Sadie.

"Good luck out in California, Riordan," Robby Collins said shaking hands. "We will pray for you and your church."

"I appreciate that, Robby. You've been a big help to us."

Emmy waited for a turn to say something to Sadie. *We've had an up and down relationship over the five and a half years you've been here, but I consider you and Riordan as friends now. Maybe not close friends, but at least we aren't enemies like I thought we might be.* Emmy smiled as Sadie stood in front of her.

"Emmy, I will be praying for you and Rebecca as you lead the team. You have been an inspiration to us over the short time we've known each other. I never would have been able to gain the support of the church without you." Sadie hugged Emmy and moved on without giving Emmy a time to respond.

Emmy waited a few minutes then left to find a seat in the sanctuary for the first service. She felt a hand on her shoulder and turned to see Liz.

"Did you say goodbye?" Emmy asked.

"I did, but we will see them after the second service. Did you have a chance to say anything?"

"Not really. Sadie did all the talking. I was trying to think of something to say, but I kept thinking about how I struggled when they first arrived."

"It's been a rocky relationship for several of the team members."

"Are things that different in California?" Emmy asked. "Dr. Behren came from California, and he was all right. He wasn't as... I don't know how to put it."

"Dr. Behren wasn't born in California like Riordan and Sadie. He grew up in Iowa, I believe."

"I hope they do well at their new church, but I can't see him as a senior pastor. I shouldn't feel like that, but I do."

"We don't always become best friends with everyone we meet, but we can always love them."

Emmy nodded and asked, "Why isn't there a potluck? We have always had one for the staff members when they leave."

"They asked not to make a big deal out of it. We have to run them up to the airport after lunch. They stayed in a hotel last night because the moving truck left in the afternoon."

"They are in a hurry to get out of SoHam, huh?"

"They have family in Pasadena, and it's home to them. We were just a place God wanted them to be for a time."

"Rebecca and I have the songs picked out for next week. I think the service will be a little different. We won't be as regimented as Riordan. He didn't always allow for last-minute changes."

"Uncle James, have you seen Mom's new Jeep? It's so cool. It can go anywhere. She took me for a ride in the woods and we almost got stuck in some mud."

"It is your father's Jeep, Kevin Michael, and I did not get stuck. I was trying out the different controls." Emmy watched Kevin dash away then looked at her half-brother. "You've lost more weight. Aren't you eating properly?"

"I haven't had much of an appetite lately."

"You are starting to look like a broomstick. I'm going to make you a basket of food to take home."

"I don't need it. It will just sit in my fridge until I throw it out."

"I'm gonna send you home with food anyway. You can either eat it or give it to homeless people. Doesn't matter."

"Taylor, look! That police car just made a u-turn and put its lights on. Someone is in trouble," Ben said on the way home from church.

Ten minutes later the SoHam officer walked back to his squad car.

"I'm sorry, Dad. I didn't realize the speed limit was twenty-five, and it didn't feel like we were going forty," Peter said.

"You have to pay attention to the road at all times," Tony said trying not to lose his cool. "You should consider yourself fortunate he's a football fan, and remembers me from my days playing for the Bears."

"Are you going to take my permit away?"

"Absolutely! No driving for you for a month!"

Ben told Mama the whole story while they ate lunch.

"I was watching him go past, and then wham! He hit the brakes and spun around. He turned on his lights but not the siren. I wish he used his siren."

"How long is Peter suspended from driving?" Mama asked.

"A month at least. After that, I will think about it," Tony answered while spooning more potato salad onto his plate.

"That's rather harsh, isn't it?"

"Mama, he needs to learn to pay attention," Tony said shaking a fork filled with food.

Mama smiled and said, "I remember the time you got a ticket for going twenty miles over the limit."

Peter looked at Mama and then his father. "Did he really, Mama?"

"When did I ever get a ticket?" Tony asked.

"You were coming home from Emmy's apartment, and trying to beat your curfew. You got pulled over and ended up being late."

"Whoa! A double whammy," Ben said. "You probably got grounded for being out late, and got a speeding ticket, too."

"I don't remember that," Tony said. He ate a bite of meat loaf and then sighed. "Okay, maybe I did get a ticket, but I learned my lesson."

"I don't remember taking your car away," Mama said.

168

"I probably needed it for football practice or something."

"Daddy, why were you at Aunt Emmy's apartment?" Noemi asked.

Sloane looked at Tony, grinned and asked, "Yes, would you care to explain that?"

"We were friends," Tony said with a shrug. "She used to help me with my homework."

"Was she smarter than you?" Taylor asked.

Sloane laughed. "I wish Emmy was here to hear your answer."

"Whose answer?" Emmy asked as she walked into the room. "Mama, can I borrow that big basket you use for casserole dishes and stuff. I'm sending Father James home with a care package. He doesn't eat properly."

"I will get it for you, dear."

Emmy looked at Sloane then Tony. "What were you guys talking about?"

"Taylor asked Dad if he was smarter than you, or if you were smarter than him when you were kids," Ben answered.

Emmy grinned and stared at Tony. "Good question, Taylor. I'm interested in hearing your father's answer."

"Fine! You were smarter than me. Happy now?"

"Daddy is so smart," Noemi said. "He knows not to mess with Aunt Emmy."

"I first joined the worship team, back in January of 2002." Emmy paused, thought about it and said, "That's eons ago. Anyway, we used printed music for everyone. We had tons of notebooks... the plastic notebooks or binders some people called them. We had to make copies and file the music away every week. That's what all those old filing cabinets were filled with."

"I would hate to have to do that now," Rebecca said. "It's so much easier to use iPads."

"Should we take a few minutes to outline our plan for the worship team, or should we go through the songs first?"

This was the first rehearsal for the team since the Schulenbergs left for California.

"We do want them to know we plan to be more flexible and listen to the Holy Spirit during the services. It might mess up the video they put on the website, but I don't want us to feel we have to stick to the schedule down to the last minute."

"I agree one hundred percent. I hate to say this, but there were times I felt Riordan resented Pastor Tyler making changes to the 'script' if you want to call it that. Riordan would time things out, and then Pastor Tyler would feel the need to change it."

"I've always appreciated the way he listens to the Spirit. Even when he gets to his sermon, he hardly ever does it the way it's written. He is always kinda winging it."

"Are you saying he should be on *Chicago Improv*?"

"What's that?" Emmy asked.

"It was a TV show. It must not be on anymore, but it was all ad-libbed. They had a basic plan for the skits, but it was all spontaneous." Rebecca waved her hands. "Whatever! It doesn't matter. Oh, Emmy, I'm so happy we are working together. I do have one request though."

"What's that?"

"Since you are in the middle of the platform, and I'm stuck over on the side behind the piano, would you do the talking. I can do it if I have to, but for now, I feel more comfortable letting you handle the transitions."

"I can do it," Emmy said. "I remember when I first joined the team and was afraid to say anything. I would sing lead, but Chase Hillman always did the talking. One Sunday he made me do it. I was really nervous, but I prayed for strength and the right words to say."

"What happened? Did God give you the right words?"

Emmy grinned and answered, "He gave me the right words, but my brain messed them up, and I sounded like a dumb kid trying to give a speech without any preparation."

Rebecca stared with a look of shock on her face.

"But I got better eventually, and now I think I do a better job. Of course, I've been singing in front of people for a long time."

"I thought you did a great job leading the service today," Kristen said as she and Emmy were rounding up the kids. "It was like old times except you didn't dance around as much."

"Thanks, Krissy. I feel like I'm too old to move around anymore."

"Do you need hip replacement surgery," Kristen teased. "Daddy is having his second one done soon, but he's seventy-nine."

"My hips work just fine," Emmy replied. "I still danced around on my last tour, but I don't feel I should do it in church."

"Do what in church?" Tony asked. "Did I miss something juicy?"

"Grow up!" Emmy said. "Kristen mentioned I didn't dance around like before."

"I did notice you were kinda glued in place. Did Pastor Tyler tell you to stand still?"

"No, but I would feel weird... never mind. How was Ben's game yesterday?"

"They won and he scored two touchdowns."

"His birthday was last Tuesday. Why didn't you guys have a party?" Emmy grabbed Kevin as he tried to get past her. "We're leaving in a minute. Stay here."

Tony shrugged and answered, "Ben said he wanted a big party next year, but he would be satisfied with cake and ice cream this year."

"Is he the biggest kid on the team?"

"He might not be the tallest, but he's definitely taller than you now."

Emmy laughed. "He sure weighs more, and he's a lot stronger than last year. He threatened to pick me up and throw me in the pool a while back."

Several other people stopped to talk to Emmy and congratulate her for doing a wonderful job.

"Mom, can we go already?" Kevin asked. "I know you and Rebecca are like the boss now, but I'm hungry and Ben and I are gonna stack some rocks for the Jeep trail later."

"I am not the 'boss' of the worship team. Rebecca and I are

co-leaders, and you are supposed to call her Pastor Rebecca now. Show some respect."

"Geez! Do I have to call you Pastor Mom?"

Emmy laughed and watched Kevin scoot away when he saw Ben and Taylor.

"Mrs. Colwell, my mom told me to tell you she liked it when you sang that hymn," Jarrett Bindley said. "I don't like those old songs, but they're all right the way you sing them."

"Thank you, Jarrett, and I like the way your hair is growing out."

"Yeah, I can't have a Mohawk anymore because Grandma yelled at Dad. I have to look normal, I guess."

"You don't have to look normal, but you do have to listen to your parents and your grandmother."

Ryan and Rebecca were ready to leave and stopped to talk to Emmy.

"You did a great job today. I really like how you extended that last song because you felt something happening."

Ryan added, "I caught your hand signal, so I knew we were doing the chorus again."

Emmy picked up nine-month-old Isaiah Deighton. "You are getting so big and more handsome every time I see you."

"He's getting to be a handful. He likes to pull himself up by the couch and walk along it," Rebecca said.

"It won't be long before you're walking and running all over the place," Emmy said as Isaiah smiled and made noises. She handed him to Ryan. "He's such a happy baby."

"He has his moments."

"All babies do," Emmy replied.

"Mom! There's Dad and Heather and Isa. Can we please go now?"

"Yes, we can go," Emmy said. "I'll see you Tuesday, Rebecca. We should spend the morning going over the songs. I think we might want to make a change. There's one Riordan chose that doesn't fit Pastor Tyler's theme."

"I agree. See you then," Rebecca said.

172

"Did Shay have the baby?" Emmy shouted into her phone. "She better have for you to call me in the middle of the night." Emmy looked at the clock. "It's two thirty, and I was sound asleep."

"Yes, Emmy, the baby is here."

"The baby better have a name and a sex."

"How's this? Karissa Mira O'Connor arrived at exactly 2:11 this morning. She and Shay are sleeping right now and doing great. Karissa weighed seven pounds on the nose and has light tufts of blonde hair. She has perfectly formed fingers and toes. Ten of each. One nose. Two blue eyes and two pink ears."

"You're so funny. Pink ears," Emmy said. "That sounds like a press release Stephanie would do for the band, but I'm happy for you guys."

"Thanks, Emmy. I'm sorry for disturbing your beauty sleep."

"It's all right," she said with a yawn. "I would have been mad if you'd waited until everyone was up to tell me. I won't tell the girls until morning because they have school and need their sleep."

"I don't suppose you want to see her today, huh?"

"Just try and keep me away, punk."

"That's Daddy Punk now, Emmy."

Chapter Twenty-One

As Tyler and Wyatt walked from the adult classroom after the Wednesday night Bible study, a group of teens passed by. Tyler noticed one hanging back and recognized him.

"Fez, right?" Tyler asked. "How are you? Still working at Darby's?"

Fez answered softly, "Yes, I am. Thanks for remembering me."

Tyler chuckled and said, "It's hard to forget that name." He looked into Fez's eyes and instantly felt the Holy Spirit telling him to talk more privately with Fez. "Do you have a minute? I know you're fairly new to the church, and I'd like to get to know you better. We could talk in the coffee shop. I have the keys and could get you a water or a pop if you'd like." Tyler noticed Fez looking around and shifting his weight back and forth. He thought it was to hide his nervousness or shyness.

"I don't have to be anywhere, but I caught a ride on the bus," Fez answered.

Tyler knew Fez worked at Darby's which was close to the river and several miles away from the church's location in Crest Ridge. "If the buses aren't running. I can give you a lift. Do you live close to Darby's?"

Fez glanced over his shoulder toward the East. "I live a few blocks on the other side of the river. The Irving Avenue and Franklin Place area. It's a long way from here."

"Which is exactly why I'll give you a ride," Tyler said knowing the area to be one of the more dangerous ones on SoHam's notorious Eastside. "Come on. I promise not to interrogate you too long."

Fez followed to the closed coffee shop in the church's foyer. Tyler grabbed two bottles of water and motioned to an empty table in the corner.

"Thanks," Fez said and sat down.

"Wyatt told me how you got the name Fez, and that your name's Anthony Rivera. Rivera is a pretty common name in SoHam. Do you have family here?"

Fez took a drink of water and then shook his head. "It's just me. I grew up in a small Wisconsin town. "

"Wyatt mentioned that. He said you went to high school in Wisconsin and came to SoHam to attend Paul Frank Junior College."

"I did, but I'd really like to go to Olivet, but it's rather expensive."

"Tell me more." Tyler watched Fez's eyes with hopes he would open up since the Spirit was still telling him this young man might need something.

"I grew up in the church and might still be living in Medford Lake, but it's a really small town and jobs are scarce. Especially if you're the only Mexican family in town," Fez said with a quirky laugh.

"There is a large Hispanic community in SoHam," Tyler said. "Do you speak Spanish?"

Fez laughed again. "Most people assume I would, but I only know a few phrases. My parents were born in Wisconsin and still live there."

"How do you like working at Darby's?"

"It's all right. I mean, Mr. Darby treats us great, and he gives us food which he doesn't have to do. It helps out, but I'm starting to get sick of hot dogs and fries."

"They still sell those homemade tamales, don't they?"

"Yes, and I like those, but they usually sell out every day."

"I can understand that. The pork ones are especially good." Tyler could tell Fez was opening up. "What's it like living there?"

Fez looked down at the table. "It's okay."

"I know that area. Be honest with me, please." He noticed Kenny Colwell approaching.

Fez took in a deep breath and looked around. "It's getting worse. The building where I live is mostly abandoned now. There's an apartment below me on the second floor that one of the local gangs is using."

Tyler waited for him to continue.

"I've heard they're using it as a meth lab, but I can't say for sure."

"Doesn't sound like the best of situations." Tyler motioned for Kenny to join them.

Kenny took a seat. "I didn't mean to eavesdrop, but I heard what you said."

"I want to move out, but I don't have enough cash right now. I spent a ton fixing the transmission on my car, and then it blew up again," Fez said. "I don't mean to sound like I need a handout or anything. I know God provides our needs."

"Sometimes God uses ordinary people to provide other's needs," Tyler said.

"You know, I might have a solution," Kenny said. "My parents have an apartment above the carriage house that sits empty all year. Dad was telling me he might look for someone to stay there just so the place is occupied."

Fez knew Kenny was a musician in a famous rock band. He stared at Kenny and shook his head. "I couldn't accept charity. No way."

"Who said anything about charity?" Kenny asked. "Dad needs someone to live there and maybe do a few things around the yard. You'd have to pay some rent, but it wouldn't be much and all the utilities are covered."

Tyler saw Fez still shaking his head but now with some emotion showing on his face.

"I couldn't," Fez repeated softly.

"Think about it," Kenny said. "I gotta grab the kids and run. Emmy drove separately and she left already."

Tyler took Fez home and, even in the dark, noticed the vacant lot filled with overgrown weeds and broken glass in the bare areas next to Fez's building. The other end of the block looked totally abandoned. The buildings were boarded up, and he saw a dozen young men loitering and talking loudly with brown bottles in hand. "I wouldn't want anyone to live here," he whispered.

Tyler was mildly surprised to see Fez back at the church the next evening. "Hi, Fez, I didn't know you were part of the worship team."

"I'm not really, but I did run sound and the computer back

home. I thought I might check out what you have if that's okay."

"I'm sure Emmy and Pastor Rebecca would love an extra tech man with experience." Tyler noticed the large, green army duffel bag behind Fez. "Is that yours?"

"Yes, I had to bring it. Sorry. I'll get it out of the way."

"It's not in the way, Fez. Does everyone always call you Fez, or do you go by Anthony, too?"

Fez laughed weakly. "My parents call me Anthony most of the time."

"Okay, I can tell something's wrong. I can see it in your eyes," Tyler said. "We should talk again." This time Tyler led Fez to his office and closed the door. He motioned for Fez to sit in one of the leather chairs and took a seat behind his cluttered desk. "I always mean to clean this up, but I never get around to it." Tyler waited then asked, "Did something happen last night?"

Fez sighed, waited a few seconds. "There were some rival gang members yelling at each other in the middle of the night. I heard some gunfire and then the window by my bed exploded. I dove over the bed and lay next to the interior wall and waited until the shooting stopped. I decided right then I wouldn't spend another night in that place. The duffel bag holds everything I own. That's why I brought it."

"I think God has provided a solution," Tyler said quietly.

"Was that offer last night for real, or was he just blowing smoke?"

Tyler chuckled. "I think you'll find that neither Kenny or Emmy ever 'blow smoke' in a situation like this. I saw them a few minutes ago. Would you like to talk to them or him?"

"I hate taking charity..."

"And trust me you aren't. Kenny meant what he said about his father needing some help around the place."

Fez closed his eyes for thirty seconds. Tyler could see his lips moving. He finally opened his eyes and looked up. "Please! I need some help."

Tyler led Fez to the music suite behind the new sanctuary. He saw Emmy talking to Ryan Deighton and asked, "Have you seen Kenny?"

Emmy looked at Tyler then Fez. "He was going to help stack those chairs and then head home. If you hurry you might catch him."

"Thanks, Emmy."

Tyler caught Kenny putting on his coat. "Got a minute?"

Kenny turned around and saw Fez. "Sure. What's up?"

Tyler explained the situation.

"I talked to Dad last night, and he agreed to let you move in right away, but he will charge you three hundred... or maybe two-fifty a month and you need to shovel the snow if we get anymore."

Tyler chuckled when he saw Fez's expression. "Don't think they're talking about a dump. The apartment above the carriage house is... Well, I'll let Kenny tell you."

"Would you mind if I take you over there in the morning? That way you could see it and decide if it will work for you."

"Sure," Fez said.

"You could crash at our house tonight," Tyler offered.

"I don't want to impose. Is there anywhere in the church I could crash just for tonight?"

"There are several couches in the Cross Fire Center," Tyler said.

Fez froze hearing the words 'cross fire' and lost all color in his normally brown tanned face.

"Sorry, bad choice of words. That's the name of the teen room upstairs in the education building," Tyler explained. "There are showers in the gym locker room."

"I don't need much," Fez said.

"Then it's settled. You can crash here tonight, and Kenny will take you to his parents' house in the morning."

Kenny nodded. "Sounds like a plan."

Shortly after eleven Kenny and Fez were headed to the Colwell house in SoHam's Raynor Park neighborhood. Kenny turned the corner onto E. Fifth Street.

"Darby's is close," Fez said.

"Emmy and I used to walk there a lot when we were kids. She lived three houses away, and we grew up together."

178

"I've read about you guys on the Internet. You're like famous rock stars, but you kinda act like normal people."

Kenny laughed and said, "I'm normal. Emmy is weird."

Fez looked at him and let a smile slowly transform his face. "I like your sense of humor."

"Thanks, please don't tell her what I said. She'll kill me."

"Our secret."

Fez gasped as Kenny turned into the driveway.

"I thought I'd come in this way instead of the alley. The carriage house is that building back there, and the apartment takes up the second floor. It's a little over a thousand square feet."

Fez nodded but couldn't speak. Kenny parked the car alongside the house and his parents walked outside.

"Dad. Mom. This is Anthony Rivera, but everyone calls him Fez. With a Z. Not like the character in that TV show. He spells his with an S." Kenny was letting his dorkiness show now.

"Fez, it's a pleasure to meet you," Carter Colwell said holding out a hand. "Call me Bob."

Fez shook hands and whispered, "It's nice to meet you, sir." He looked up at the two-story brick house then over his shoulder at the equally impressive two-story brick carriage house.

"You must be hungry," Elly Colwell said. "I have some lunch ready if you'd like."

"Could I show Fez the apartment first, Mom?" Kenny asked.

"Of course. Come into the house if you'd like. I have plenty."

Kenny started walking toward the carriage house. He didn't hear Fez coming, so he turned around. "It's this way."

"Sure," Fez said. "You're kidding about the rent, right?"

Kenny smiled then shrugged. "You haven't seen the inside yet. It might be a dump." *Shoot! I shouldn't have said that. It sounded like I was bragging.*

Kenny opened the service door and led the way up the wide stairs. He unlocked the door and held it open for Fez. "It used to be filled with junk when Emmy and I were kids. She was scared to come up here, but she was only like eight at the time."

179

"You really have known her a long time." Fez said without realizing it might make Emmy appear older than she was. "Two fifty a month for this?"

Kenny nodded.

"What's the catch? You could rent this for ten times that."

"Maybe, but Dad is particular about who lives here. He would rather have someone he trusts than someone who could afford more rent. You know what I mean?"

"Not really? You don't know me at all. Why me?" Fez asked choking back his emotions.

Kenny waved a hand. "Aw, Dad's a good judge of character." Kenny gave Fez the tour. "Don't tell Emmy I told you, but this is where we spent our wedding night."

"Get out!"

"Swear," Kenny said.

"You probably shouldn't tell that to people."

Kenny shrugged. "We kept it quiet at the time, but word got out over the years. Now everyone in SoHam knows."

Fez tapped his jaw and said, "The pictures on the walls above some of the booths at Darby's. They're you and the band. I just realized that."

"Yeah, and the little girl in the photos on stage with us is Emmy. She was fourteen at the time. Our girls are thirteen now. Time flies," Kenny said. "The bathroom is in there and you can see the kitchen and great room..."

"This is where the band started, right? I've read about that. This is the place!" he said slowly with his voice gaining volume with each word.

"Yeah, but it didn't look this nice back then. It was just one big room."

"This is the place!" he said again as the implication set in.

"You okay, Fez?" Kenny asked.

"God certainly provides, doesn't He?" Fez said choking back his emotions.

"I finished cleaning my room and all my dirty laundry is downstairs," Heather said Saturday afternoon.

"Thank you, Heather," Emmy replied as she worked on the outline for her next book in the family room.

"Mom, did I tell you about the text I got?" Heather asked knowing she hadn't.

"What text, sweetie?" Emmy asked without looking away from her laptop.

"It's kinda a late notice, but Drew texted me asking if I could come to the teen party at the church tonight. He said he would pick me up. Can I go?"

"Okay," Emmy answered though distracted.

Heather grinned and turned to leave.

"Wait one second, young lady," Emmy said. "He's picking you up? Who exactly is Drew? Do I know him?"

"He's Serena's older brother."

"The Serena who is friends with Phoebe Hammond?" Emmy asked closing her laptop and sitting up straight.

"No, she's my age," Heather said.

"How old is Drew?"

"Sixteen, I think," Heather answered.

Emmy jumped up, pointed at Heather and said, "A sixteen-year-old boy wants to take you to a party. Are you nuts?" Emmy's voice rose an octave. "No way you are going. Out of the question."

"Why not? He's from church."

"Doesn't matter. Sixteen is too old for you, and you know the rules. You can't date until you're sixteen, and then only in a group to church events."

"You just made that up. You've never mentioned that silly rule before, and this is at the church."

"You are thirteen! Talk to me again when you're eighteen. Maybe I will allow you to date then."

"Eighteen! Now who's nuts?" Heather stomped away muttering to herself. She stamped her feet as much as possible going upstairs.

Emmy sighed, sat down and opened her laptop. *I have to finish this before dinner.*

"Isa, where is your sister? It's time for dinner?" Emmy asked as Isabella and Kevin set the table in the breakfast nook.

Isabella shrugged without answering. Kevin stared outside.

"Did you hear me?" Emmy asked. "Please tell Heather it's time to eat."

Isabella looked at Kevin. He looked back and shrugged. Emmy saw them looking at each other.

"Okay! What's going on. You look as guilty as Richard Nixon."

"We can't tell you," Kevin said drawing a nasty look from Isabella.

"What can't you tell me?" Emmy asked.

"If I tell you what I can't tell you then I've told you what I can't tell you, Mom."

"Where is Heather?" Emmy asked loudly.

Kenny walked into the kitchen. "What's the yelling about?"

"Do you know where your daughter is?" Emmy asked.

Kenny looked at Isabella and instantly realized Emmy must be asking about Heather. "I haven't seen her for a couple hours. She was upstairs the last I knew."

"Kevin, run upstairs and tell her to come here this moment."

Kevin looked at Isabella again. His bottom lip began to quiver.

Isabella said, "He can't, Mom, because she left."

"We were supposed to keep her secret until death," Kevin whispered.

"Where is she, Isa?" Kenny asked. He knew nothing about the party invite.

"She might have gone to Uncle Tony's house," Isabella admitted.

Emmy called Tony's cell phone and as soon as he answered, she yelled, "Send Heather home immediately!"

"Hello to you, too, Emmy, but you know I can't do that."

"Why not?"

"Well, because she rode with Sloane and the kids to the teen thing at church. Sloane will bring them back after she gets some groceries."

"I told her she couldn't go!"

182

"Sloane?"

Emmy rolled her eyes. "No, doofus! Heather!"

"Oh, she said you told her she could, but would need a ride."

Kevin looked at Isabella and whispered, "Busted."

"She lied, and I'm gonna murder her!" Emmy screamed.

"I wondered why Isa wasn't coming."

Kenny, Isabella and Kevin watched as Emmy grabbed her purse and keys and raced to the garage without a word. A minute later they heard tires squealing as Emmy left in the Jeep.

"Did you cover for Heather?" Kenny asked.

"She told me I had to or else she'd throw all my electronics in the bathtub," Kevin said.

"Isa, do you know what's going on?" Kenny asked calmly.

Isabella explained about the teen event and the invite from Drew MacNeill.

Emmy made it to the church without being arrested for driving-like-a-maniac, parked the Jeep right in front, sprinted inside, passed two of the maintenance staff without acknowledging their wave, and raced to the second floor Cross Fire Teen Center. She pushed open the door loud enough to bang it against the wall and startle everyone inside.

"Heather Rose Colwell! You are grounded for all eternity and maybe even longer!"

Brenda Wiley, the wife of the teen pastor, turned to Emmy and asked, "Did you come to help?" She flicked her long red hair over her shoulder. "We could use the extra hands."

Emmy looked around the room. She saw several teen girls with Brenda on one side of the room placing bottles of water, toothbrushes and other items into small bags and then into larger boxes. She turned and saw a few teenage boys on the other side with Pastor Daryl doing something similar. "Help with what?"

"Hi, Emmy," Pastor Daryl said approaching her. "You must have heard about the earthquake and the fires in Costa Rica. I know it was a last minute thing, but some of the teens wanted to help. We're putting together crisis care kits to send to Kansas City."

183

"Earthquake? Fires? Crisis care kits?" Emmy muttered softly. She looked for Heather and saw her trying to hide behind one of the other girls.

"It won't take long if we have many hands to help," Brenda said. "We promised to order pizzas later."

Emmy walked to the table on the girls' side of the room and watched as the teens chatted away while slowly accomplishing the goal. She looked at Heather, who turned away with her head down.

"I will talk to you later," Emmy mouthed.

An hour later the pizzas arrived.

"I'm sorry, Mommy," Heather whispered as she followed Emmy outside.

Emmy unlocked the Jeep and said, "Get in."

"I'm still in trouble, huh?"

"What do you think? You lied to me, and totally disregarded my desires."

"Sorry, but it was for a good cause."

Emmy shook her head. "Doesn't matter, Heather. You lied to Sloane, to me, probably to Brenda and Daryl. Why did you do that?"

"I wanted to help," Heather said.

"Really? Or did you want to be with that boy?"

"Both, I suppose."

"He's sixteen."

"Daddy is three and a half years older than you," Heather said. Not the first time she had used that as an excuse.

"How many times do I have to refute that argument? Your father and I were good friends at that age. Lifelong friends you could say."

"Did your parents let you go places with Daddy?"

Emmy thought of the countless times she was allowed to join Kenny and his parents on family outings. She remembered even going on vacation with them.

"I know they did."

"Heather, I wish I could say I never lied to my parents, but I can't. That doesn't make it all right for you to do what I did. I disobeyed my parents more times than I can remember, and I wish

184

I could change that. I can't." She looked at Heather and saw herself at that age. "Which boy was Drew?"

"He was wearing the North Park hoodie. His father teaches there, and his mom works in a bank or something. They started coming to church last month."

"Did you know what the teens were going to do tonight?"

"Not exactly. Drew said something about pizzas and Bandaids and toothbrushes, but I just wanted to see him."

"And be seen with him," Emmy added. "I know it can make you feel important and 'cool' to your friends if an older boy shows an interest. That can de a dangerous thing, Heather. Three years is a big difference at your age."

"But Grandma and Grandpa must have trusted Daddy if they let you hang out together all the time. Weren't they worried he might try something?"

"I'm sure they were at times, but he and I were just friends then." Emmy grinned and said, "Have you seen pictures of your father at sixteen?"

"Maybe."

"You have and his hair wasn't as long as now. Most of the time his ears weren't covered."

Heather smiled. "You always tease him about his ears."

"It's not as bad now, but back then he looked so weird with those ears sticking out. He looked like Dumbo at times."

Heather laughed. "It's a good thing his hair covers them now, huh?"

"I used to tell him to staple them to his head."

Emmy told Heather about more times she and Kenny did things together. Soon they were both giggling and laughing.

"Let's go home," Emmy said. She started the Jeep and left the parking lot.

"Am I still grounded?" Heather asked.

"Oh, yes! But there is good news."

"What?" Heather asked.

"You may appeal for parole in twenty years. Until then you are confined to your room."

"That's not funny," Heather said.

185

"I didn't intend it to be," Emmy answered.

"In twenty years I'll be too old to care about boys," Heather said with a sigh.

"Krissy, what are your plans for today? You probably told me, but I forgot. You and the kids aren't going to be alone for Thanksgiving, are you?"

"No, Wyatt and his parents will be here. I am making everything."

"Are you sure that's wise? Wyatt might not like it if you poison his parents," Emmy teased.

"Are you going to tease me about my culinary skills my entire life? I have learned how to cook over the years."

"Sorry, I know you have. Where do his parents live? Pennsylvania, right?"

"No, that's where Wyatt and Evie lived after college. His parents still live in Ann Arbor, Michigan. Thomas lives not too far away. That is Wyatt's brother."

"I should have remembered that," Emmy said. "Hey! Have you started your Christmas shopping? You might not have much time after the wedding and it's less than a month away. Christmas, I mean. The wedding is only nine days away. Are you getting anxious?"

"I am not getting anxious," Kristen said as she turned on the oven. "I have not started, but I will probably order everything online. The kids gave me a list. They were very specific and even put Amazon links to everything."

"Smart thinking. Kevin gave me a three page list. I handed it right back and told him to hire an editor. No way he needs all that stuff."

"Do you still make them donate their old toys to make room for new ones?"

"If I didn't, we'd have to add on another wing," Emmy answered.

Chapter Twenty-Two

"Are you ready, Kristen?" Emmy asked. "This is the first time you've gotten married in a church."

"You are such a stinker. How can you joke at a time like this?" Kristen checked the mirror for the umpteenth time in the last five minutes.

"I'm not joking. You got married to John at home. I was there, remember?"

Kristen looked at Emmy's feet. "I remember you wore sneakers to the reception."

"Those other shoes hurt my feet."

Someone knocked quietly on the door and Emmy opened it.

"Is Mommy ready?" Grace asked. "Grandma says it's time to start. She's going to push Grandpa to his seat and then move the wheelchair."

"I'm ready," Kristen said. "Where is Zach?"

"I'm here," he answered setting down the latest Starfighter model Wyatt gave him the night before.

Emmy walked out of the room where years before she had waited before getting married. "Are the guys standing out there?"

Zach peeked into the old sanctuary. "They're there. Uncle Tony waved at me."

"We better get moving before your mother runs back here," Emmy said. "I have to go first, and then you and Grace walk your mother to the front. Understand, Zach?"

"We got this, Aunt Emmy. You made us practice a hundred times last night."

Emmy took another look at Kristen and hugged her tightly.

"You better not be crying when I walk out there," Kristen warned.

"I won't. Promise."

Zach turned to Grace. "Bet you ten dollars she will be bawling like a baby."

"I'm not stupid, Zach. Why would anyone take a bet like that. It would be like giving your money to a bald eagle or a baby polar bear."

"Were you watching the Nature Channel again?" Kristen asked.

"I love bald eagles," Grace said.

"I love hawks because they dive bomb just like a Starfighter."

"Okay, it's time to be serious," Emmy said. "Remember to walk slow."

Emmy started down the center aisle of the old sanctuary of Crest Ridge United Nazarene. *This is the first time I've done this in years.* She smiled at Phoebe Hammond and Lily Robertson. *You two are still so cute.* She glanced to her right and spotted Kenny and her kids. *I am so lucky to have such a wonderful family.* She saw Pastor Tyler, Wyatt and Tony smiling on the platform. *Don't you dare make a face at me, Tony Bertucci. I will make your life miserable if you do.* She reached the steps, climbed up and moved to her left. She looked back, saw Zach and Grace on either side of Kristen and began to lose it. She bit her lip hard to maintain composure. *I will not cry! I will not cry! Oh, crap, my makeup is going to be ruined.* She looked at Tony and saw his chin quiver.

Zach and Grace stood beside their mother on the platform as Pastor Tyler greeted everyone.

"Please allow me to pray to start this ceremony." He prayed, looked at Kristen and the kids, chuckled and then asked, "Who gives this woman away?"

"We do!" Zach and Gracie said loud enough to be heard in the back of the sanctuary. They ran down the stairs and sat beside their grandparents.

Tyler continued the ceremony.

I'm glad you didn't ask me to sing, Krissy. I would have looked silly trying to sing and crying at the same time. She looked at Kristen and Wyatt and sighed. *I thought John was the perfect man for you, but he screwed up royally.* Her mind continued to roam until she heard Kristen's voice.

"I need the ring, Emmy."

"Sorry, I was... lost in thought."

Soon, Pastor Tyler introduced the new couple and Wyatt and Kristen began walking out.

"Have we done this before, brat?" Tony asked as he offered his arm to Emmy. "It feels like deja vu all over again."

"Shut up! If you're thinking we were 'posed to get married, you got it all wrong. We're distant cousins, remember?"

"I remember."

"You better not forget."

"I won't."

"Let's hurry so I can talk to Kristen before the crowd gets to her." Emmy tugged on his arm and they rushed out of the sanctuary.

"What are you going to do, Em?"

"I'm going to tease her about robbing the cradle. You do know Wyatt is four years younger than Krissy, right?"

"I knew he was younger," Tony said.

Emmy hugged Kristen and whispered about the cradle robbing.

"Like it makes a difference at our age," Kristen said.

"Congratulations, Wyatt, you did a great job with the vows," Tony said, "and don't listen to Emmy."

Eventually, the receiving line trickled to only a few people and the wedding party headed to the all-purpose room for the reception.

"Do I have to walk next to you," Emmy asked looking up at Tony.

"I'm not going to carry you."

"You used to carry me around," she whispered. "You used to hang me from the ceiling."

He laughed and replied, "I should have left you there."

The small wedding party sat together at the head table along with Tyler and Liz.

Kristen made a face at the Bertucci boys because they kept banging their plastic silverware on the table.

"Kiss him!" Noemi and the twins yelled.

Wyatt smiled at Kristen and said, "We have to do what they ask."

"Okay, but I would like to eat at some point."

189

Later, after Kristen and Wyatt cut the cake, Emmy maneuvered Kristen away from the crowd and asked, "Why did you guys have such a short engagement? I know why Bobby and Shay did. Have you..."

"Emmy! How can you even ask? Wait!" Kristen held up a hand. "You are asking because you are so curious and just have to know, and the answer is we didn't want to wait until after the holidays. We wanted to be a family before Christmas. Not because of sex."

"Where are you spending the night? I know the kids are staying with Tony and Sloane."

"If you lean close, I will tell you, but you cannot tell anyone else because we are keeping it a secret."

Emmy giggled and moved closer to Kristen. "Tell me."

"Promise you will keep our secret?"

Emmy raised a hand. "I promise."

"Okay, we have made arrangements to spend the night..."

"Where! Tell me."

"In your nanny suite," Kristen said.

"What? No one told me."

Kristen rolled her eyes and walked away.

Chapter Twenty-Three

"I just got a text from Matt Sullivan about Annie," Emmy announced to the family at breakfast.

"Did she have her baby?" Isabella asked.

"Why else would Matt be texting Mom?" Kevin asked sarcastically.

"Be nice, or else you'll lose another day's privileges," Kenny warned.

"She had a baby boy," Emmy read from the text.

"We know that, Mom. You told us months ago she was having a boy," Heather said.

"Kinda small. Only five pounds and two ounces."

"Is that smaller than we were?" Isabella asked.

"You were both smaller. That's why you had to stay in the hospital so long," Emmy explained.

"Em, what did they name him?" Kenny asked.

"Samuel Liam Sullivan. Liam is Annie's grandfather. Samuel Liam. I like it. I bet they call him Sammy."

Isabella set her glass of apple juice down. "Was he born with Down Syndrome? Does he look normal or can you tell?"

"There isn't a photo, but he probably looks like any other baby."

"Are you gonna go to the hospital?" Kevin asked stabbing another piece of bacon from the platter.

"Annie wants me to come this morning."

Emmy parked in the deck and hurried inside. She got a visitor pass and made her way to room 4012. She knocked on the door and stepped inside.

Matt smiled at her. "Annie was wondering how long it would take you to get here. You just missed my in-laws and Alanna, but Grandpa Liam is bringing Keyshon. He should be here in a few minutes."

"I haven't seen her grandpa for several years. Oh, I did see him at Mom's funeral," Emmy said. "How is Annie? She looks asleep."

"I was just closing my eyes, Emmy. Come and sit by me."

Annie held baby Samuel in her arms while he slept.

"I won't stay long, but I wanted to see you. How are you and Samuel doing?"

"I'm tired, but feel okay. Samuel is perfect even though the world might not see it that way. I will always remember our talk. Who knows what might have happened if you hadn't convinced me to have him."

"God will provide every need you and Samuel have."

Annie grinned and said, "I'll hold you to that."

They both turned to look as they heard a voice.

"Mom! Can I come in? Grandpa said you might be feeding him."

"Come on in, Keyshon," Matt said.

Emmy watched as Keyshon Sullivan cautiously walked to the opposite side of the bed. *Why was I expecting him to look like Keyshon Franklin. That wouldn't be possible because Annie and Mace are step-brother and sister. They named you Keyshon to honor Mace's little brother. You're totally Irish, and it shows.*

"Keyshon, do you remember Emmy?" Annie asked.

He nodded. "You're mom's old friend from high school. I have one of your books at home. It's okay, but I like Mom's better."

Emmy grinned.

"Keyshon!"

"It's okay. Just between you and me, your mother is a much better writer than me," Emmy whispered.

Liam O'Dell tapped the floor with his cane. "Are you decent, child? I don't want to disturb you if you are feeding my new grandson."

"Grandpa! You can come in no matter what," Annie said with a wide smile. "Do you want to hold him. He's asleep."

"Ah! Let me sit down to hold him." Grandpa took baby Samuel and held him tenderly. "How are you, Mrs. Colwell? Have you been behaving?" he asked sternly.

"I haven't gotten a detention in years, Principal O'Dell," she said with a giggle. "I talked to Mace earlier this year.

"He is the vice-principal now. Did you know that?"

192

"I didn't until he told me."

"Did he mention he and Erin have four kids?"

"Four? He didn't mention that."

"Kendra is the oldest. She's nine and the youngest is not quite two. She's as pretty as a picture." He smiled at his newest grandchild. "You will have to meet your cousins someday."

"I'm happy for Mace. He and Annie are step-brother and step-sister since Detective O'Dell and Mrs. Franklin got married several years ago," Emmy said. "He talked about school and basketball, but not a lot about his family." *Why do I detect some tension between Liam and Annie?*

Liam stared at Annie for a moment. "He probably didn't mention that my stubborn granddaughter and Erin were roommates through college and now they are barely civil to each other."

"I have my reasons, Grandpa," Annie said. "Let's not talk about that now."

Liam grunted at Annie, faced Emmy and said, "I read your latest book."

"What did you think?"

He grinned and said, "Absolutely scandalous! That young girl should have been paddled for getting into so much trouble. She reminded me of two other young ladies who were quite mischievous in their youth."

Annie smiled and put a finger to her mouth. "Grandpa, Ruby can't be based on me or Emmy because we were innocent virgins in high school."

"That may be true, but you were definitely devilish at times."

Matt laughed and nodded. "I certainly can't argue with you, Grandpa Liam. Annie was undeniably exasperating at times, but she was innocent about sex. No matter what everyone thought. I can't make the same claim."

"I was until you came along," Annie said.

Emmy listened to their frank conversation. *How can they talk about that in front of their son?*

"I can't say anything about Emmy, but I suspect she wasn't much different than you," Matt said to his wife.

"How is retirement treating you, Principal O'Dell. Do you still like to fish?" Emmy asked.

"I will not answer your questions until you stop calling me that. You may call me Liam, or Grandpa Liam, young lady."

"Yes, Liam, and you may call me Emmy."

"I enjoy every day of retirement to the best of my ability, and that includes fishing." He looked at young Keyshon. "The only difference is now I go fishing with a different Keyshon."

"You were very close to him, weren't you?"

"He and I were best buds, and I miss him just as much now as when he first passed."

"I hope you and Samuel will be best buds one day," Emmy said. She smiled at Liam, leaned over and kissed his cheek. "I pray you and Samuel catch a lot of fish together."

Chapter Twenty-Four

"You are such a stinker!" Kristen hollered before Emmy could even say hello. "I cannot believe it."

"Why am I a stinker? I didn't do anything," Emmy replied. "Merry Christmas, Kristen."

Kristen sighed and continued, "Merry Christmas to you, too, Emmy. Do you remember what you told me after the wedding?"

"I don't remember my exact words, but I probably teased you about your wedding night."

"You did. You were acting like we were kids again."

"I was so happy for you."

Kristen heard some noise in the background. "Where are you?"

"In the bathroom. Why?"

"Did you just flush the toilet?" Kristen asked loudly.

"Yes."

"You are a double stinker! How can you talk to me while using the bathroom?"

"We weren't facetiming, Krissy. You can't see me." Emmy washed her hands, turned off the light, walked across the room and sat on the edge of the bed. "Where are you right now?"

"In the kitchen making coffee and toast. Do you always take your phone to the bathroom with you? No! Don't answer that. I don't want that picture in my mind."

"Don't burn the toast," Emmy teased.

"You are so funny."

"Wyatt is the perfect man for you in this season of your life,"

"What is that suppose to mean?"

"You're older now..."

"So are you."

"Yes, and my life is changing. We both have different needs and have new priorities from when we were first married."

"Yeah! All you wanted when you and Kenny got married was to have sex all the time. You were insufferable."

Emmy laughed and added, "I'm not quite as bad as I used to be."

"You are still... Oh, never mind."

"You still haven't told me why I'm a stinker unless it was for teasing you. How has the sex been, by the way?"

"I am not talking to you about my sex life. Not ever again."

"I hope you had a good time on your honeymoon," Emmy said and then waited for a response. "Did you hear me?"

"I heard you, and it was very enjoyable."

"I bet."

"You can be such a child at times, Emily Colwell."

"Are Wyatt and Zachary getting along better now?" Emmy asked. "I know Gracie loves him."

"They are. Wyatt talked to him about not replacing his father, but that he expected Zach to show respect."

"I think in time Zach and Wyatt will be best buds. It's not easy for teenagers under the best of circumstances. A divorce is a lot for them to handle."

"Grace says she misses John, but Zach doesn't mention him anymore. Not around me at least."

"Zach told Kevin a while back that he would never change his last name to Pearson. He would always be Zachary Randolph."

"I told the kids I would never expect them to change their name as soon as Wyatt and I got serious."

"I never thought they would. It was different when Tony and Sloane adopted Peter and Dotty. They were young and it made sense to change their name."

"I can smell the coffee," Wyatt said as he stepped into the kitchen. He hugged Kristen and kissed her.

"I heard that. Are you guys making out?" Emmy asked.

"He gave me a kiss. We are not... Oh, why do I even talk to you about things."

"Because you love me, and we are best friends," Emmy answered. "Why am I a stinker? Tell me."

"I'll be in the family room," Wyatt said. "You can talk to Emmy in private."

Kristen kissed him and waited for him to leave the kitchen.

196

"You teased me about getting pregnant and guess what?"

Emmy's eyes opened wide. "Are you telling me..."

"Yes! I knew it right away. I could just tell."

"Did you pee on a stick?"

Kristen sighed and said, "You have such a delicate way of asking. But, yes, three times."

Emmy jumped into the air and then plopped onto the bed. "I can't believe it. This is a wonderful Christmas surprise."

"You are not the only one who was surprised."

"Didn't you use protection or something?"

Kristen stared at her phone.

"Duh! Silly me. Obviously you guys didn't."

"I will be forty when the baby is born. That is too old to have a child."

"Mom was almost forty when she had me," Emmy said. She sat on the edge of the bed again. "Who have you told?"

"Just Wyatt and now you. I haven't told the kids or my parents or anyone."

"I know those tests are a lot more accurate now, but isn't it too early to tell for sure?"

"Not according to the Internet. I checked."

"I hope you have a girl," Emmy said in her childlike voice.

"At my age I pray for a healthy baby."

"Can I tell Kenny and the girls?"

"No! You cannot tell a soul, Emily Olivia. You have to keep this a secret. I know that will be difficult, but I want to wait until I see my doctor. Can you do that?"

"I promise. Scout's honor." Emmy held up a hand in salute.

"You were never a Girl Scout, Em."

"True, but that's still a sacred oath," she said and then giggled. "I can't believe you're pregnant. You are gonna get so big..."

"Thank you ever so much."

"Oh, Krissy, I didn't mean it like that. What did Wyatt say?"

"He was speechless at first, but then he hugged me and said he has always wanted to be a father."

"He will make a good, good father," Emmy said and began humming a tune.

"I suppose I will have to find a way to work from home after the baby is born."

"There are plenty of companies allowing employees to work from home now." Emmy snapped her fingers. "In fact, I bet you could work for Brady's company. I was talking to Diane, and she mentioned they were looking for someone who could coordinate travel plans and stuff. You would be perfect for that."

"I appreciate the suggestion, but I don't want to take advantage of Brady and Diane. Liberty Manufacturing is slowly progressing into the twenty-first century. I am hoping they will allow me to work from home."

"Are you going to keep working for now?"

"I have to. We have expenses like normal people."

"We have bills to pay, too," Emmy replied.

"I was not implying you are not normal, Em. Wait! You are far from normal if the definition of normal is average."

"Thanks, I think."

"I hope God gives me the right words to use when I tell Zach and Grace about this."

"He always does, Krissy. He knows everything about the baby. He's always known you and Wyatt would be parents," Emmy said, paused and added, "I think God wants you to have a girl and name her Emily Kristen."

"Don't you dare expect me to name my baby after you."

"I'm just teasing."

"I know. I better go. The kids will be up soon and will want to open presents."

"Yeah, tell me. I better put the gifts under the tree so they'll know Santa has been here."

"Emmy, they know Santa isn't real," Kristen said. "Oh, wait! It's you who still believes in Santa Claus."

"Ha! Ha! I'll let you go, and thanks for the Christmas surprise. I'll keep it a secret until you tell me I can announce it to the world."

"Bye and Merry Christmas, Em."

"Merry Christmas and I just thought of something."

Kristen heard Emmy laughing. "Tell me."

"At least now you guys don't have to worry about using protection."

Kristen shook her head and ended the call.

"Who were you talking to, Em?" Kenny asked as he and the kids entered the bedroom.

Emmy clutched a pillow to her chest and bit her lip.

"Who was on the phone, Mommy?" Isabella asked. "Was it Grandma and Grandpa?"

Emmy stood up still holding the pillow. "It was Krissy."

Everyone waited for more but Emmy remained quiet.

"What did Aunt Kristen say?" Heather asked.

"Nothing important," Emmy said with a hand behind her back.

Kenny knew that tone of voice and her actions meant something.

"Can we open presents before breakfast this year?" Kevin asked.

"Sounds like a good idea," Kenny said. "I'll meet you downstairs in just a minute."

The kids raced away.

"Emmy!" Kenny drew out her name.

"It's a secret, and I can't tell you."

"I have a way of making you talk," he said menacingly but with a grin.

She smiled back. "That sounds like fun, but it won't work. I still can't tell you."

"Fine!" He turned his back and headed for the door. "You can keep your secret for now, but I'll find out eventually."

She grinned and thought, *Yeah, in about nine months.*

Check out these other titles by the author. Visit the website:
kennethleemcgee.com

The Emmy's Story Series
1. We Were 'posed to Get Married
2. One Of The Guys
3. A New Friend
4. Did You Like the Ravioli Tonight?
5. Completely and Forever: A Wedding
6. It's Time To Go!
7. How Difficult Can It Be?
8. Forever... Isabella... Forever
9. The Forgettable Year
10. Turning Thirty
11. Hello, I'm James
12. Remember The Struggle
13. But God! I Write Songs
14. A Lifelong Dream
15. Gideon's Tree
16. New Priorities

The Annie Mercer O'Dell Series
1. Roosevelt High
2. North Park College
3. Smoky Mountain Summer

Rex Ford & Clay Horn Adventures
1. The Amazing Adventures of Rex Ford & Clay Horn

Stand Alone Books
1. Growing Up In Kinmundy Junction
2. Grandpa, Lions and Kitty Cats: A Collection Of Short Stories For Children Of All Ages